LOVE AND MONSTERS

A Collection of Erotic Horror

OTHER BOOKS BY

KAREN E. TAYLOR

THE VAMPIRE LEGACY SERIES:

Blood Red Dawn

Thirst

Crave

Hunger

CELLAR

MEXICAN MOON and Other Stories

LOVE AND MONSTERS

A Collection of Erotic Horror

Karen E. Taylor

PROVENANCE

"Gestation" was published on the *Dark Fluidity* website, October 2003.

"The Mirrored Image" first saw print in *Love Bites*, published by Masquerade Books, 1995.

"Obsession" first saw print in *No Other Tribute*, published by Masquerade Books, 1996.

"The Presence" first saw print in *Seductive Spectres*, published by Masquerade Books, 1996

"With the Wings of Angels" first saw print in *Fangs and Angel Wings*, published by Wildside Press, November 2003.

Cover design copyright ©2016 by Melanie Fletcher.

Karen E. Taylor
Alexandria, VA
http://www.karenetaylor.com

TABLE OF CONTENTS

GESTATION 1

THE MIRRORED IMAGE 15

OBSESSION 39

THE PRESENCE 51

WITH THE WINGS OF ANGELS 109

GESTATION

Hands. She becomes aware of the hands first. Hands probing and examining. Hands with their latex-covered caress, checking her pulse spots, touching her forehead, pressing her knees apart, positioning her feet. Clinical, but familiar. Struggling to place the touch, her mind grasps at these hands, reaching out to fall just inches short of connection. Then the warmth of the hands is replaced by the sharp cold sting of metal, penetrating and piercing. She feels pain.

Her own hands clasp into fists and attempt to break free of their restraints, succeed only in drumming on the metal surface to which she is affixed.

"She's coming to."

"Then give her more."

Ah, that voice, she knows that voice. It is as familiar as the hands.

"But she's already had more than three times—"

"Give her more."

And the voice and the hands dissolve into darkness.

Magda woke, rolled over and looked at the sleeping form of her lover. Evan Thomas was a brilliant man; truly brilliant, as well as powerful, arrogant and cruel. The combination pleased Magda well. Especially, she thought with a rueful smile, the cruelty.

It was not that she sought to be hurt. The presence or absence of pain made no difference in her quest for pleasure. What mattered most was being mastered; only the feeling of being completely powerless in the grip of another could give her satisfaction. It had taken her many long and lonely years of experimentation to understand her needs. Magda needed to be overwhelmed, needed to be subdued; she craved the ultimate seduction she'd made possible for so many, but that no man or woman had yet given her.

Before Evan she had feared her needs would forever go unsatisfied. And forever for Magda was much too long a time. But with one look, she had known instantly—this man would change her life. The certainty that he'd also known it showed in his eyes, his walk, the possessive way he appropriated the space next to her that night at the crowded bar.

"I've seen you here before, haven't I?"

Magda shrugged and raised a delicately shaped eyebrow. For an opening line, it wasn't much.

"Yes, I have," the man continued, unaffected by her scorn. "I have watched you. So many nights, so many men. No, not men. Boys. So many pretty boys. And what did they do for you but leave you hungry for more? You should try a man of substance, a man with presence and power."

To punctuate his words he took her hand and pressed it onto his upper thigh. She could feel the heat of his skin through his jeans, feel the muscles of his leg. He moved her hand again, impatiently, and she felt the jump of his penis beneath her fingers. Her breath caught in her throat.

"We will dance first," he said, "and then you will come with me."

When they danced, he held her close with one arm, while holding her arms behind her back with his other. Surprised by his sheer aggressiveness, Magda allowed this familiarity and abandoned herself to his control. Her reactions were instinctive; the almost instant surrender of her mind and body to him was sweet, intoxicating.

And later, when he had rendered her helpless, bound, gagged and blindfolded, when he had taken her and coaxed and teased and tortured her beyond her most secret dreams of ecstasy, she knew she would never have another lover like him. With each penetration, each new invasion of her body, he had bound her to him, more certainly than the ropes and scarves holding her as his captive.

This is not love, Magda thought, one could not call it love. "But it's better this way," she whispered, stretching for a second before wrapping herself around Evan's warm body, "much better."

"I know what you are," he had said to her after their fifth night together.

Magda sighed. He was such a wonderful lover and this moment had come too soon. "Really, Evan?" Wondering what had given away her secret, she ran a sharpened nail down the center of his chest to his stomach and stopped at the junction of penis and groin; a knife held to a neck. It must have been the gags, she thought, and the distinctive fang marks I left on them. But she held back her anger, and held on to her hopes that she was wrong. "And what am I?"

"You are a dream. A fantasy. The illusionary creature I've searched for, my entire life." He picked up the threatening hand and kissed the tip of her fingernail. "You are the answer to my prayers."

She laughed. "You pray?"

He didn't return the laugh. "I am a scientist, but I still believe in the presence of some other existence, some something that cannot be proved by science. Yet. And you are my proof."

Magda had searched his eyes for confirmation of her own beliefs. And had seen nothing, then or since, to make her think Evan knew her secret.

Five years, Magda realized as she continued to watch Evan sleep, we've been together for five whole years. Not a long time, especially by the standards of her lifetime, but for Magda it was a record. Never before had a man kept her so satisfied and so intrigued. Like Scheherazade, he always did something to postpone his ending. As if sensing a potential boredom, he would introduce some new sexual game; featuring himself in the dominant role, of course, with her as the submissive. And although she was always bound in some way as well as gagged and blindfolded, his variations seemed endless.

He had spent one week entirely focused on her feet. Stroking them with fingers, or feathers, or pricking them with pins with her splayed out on the bed, her arms and legs each tightly fastened to a bed post. He would lick them, sucking on each toe with excruciating slowness, making her squirm and whimper through the gag. He would rub himself against her soles, order her to bring him to climax with nothing but her feet.

The next week it had been her breasts. Biting and suckling, pinching and tweaking, nipple rings and clamps, so very many degrees of scintillation, Evan played rhapsodies on a familiar theme and her body echoed them back to him.

"I think you must have a list of fetishes a mile long," Magda said one late evening as she prepared to leave, "what will you do when you get to the end?"

Evan laughed. "If we ever get to the end of my list, I suppose one of us will have to leave. Or die." He glared at her for a second. "Are you complaining?"

"Never, my lord and master. I am yours to command." She had given a quick curtsey when saying these words, then had dropped a quick kiss on his cheek and she was gone, leaving with a smile and a hunger for their next meeting.

"Perfect." Magda spoke the words quietly. "You are the perfect lover." *Except eventually you will grow old and tired. And then it will be over.* She sighed loudly and Evan woke.

"What time is it?"

"About four, I think."

"Oh. And you'll be leaving soon, no doubt. Did you sleep well?" His voice held a concern totally uncharacteristic of him.

"Not bad," Magda admitted, oddly flustered by his question, "although I had a strange dream."

"Oh? What was it about?" Evan got up and went into the bathroom.

"I don't quite remember. It was a dream. Sort of familiar, like a dream I've dreamt before. You know how dreams are. They make sense at the time, then what little meaning they have seems to fade away." She heard the stream of his urine splash into the toilet. Start, stop, start, stop. Another sign of the inevitable aging process she hated.

He came out of the bathroom, naked, scratching his side absentmindedly. "Was I in it?"

Magda frowned then shrugged. "I can't remember. It doesn't matter."

"No, I don't suppose it does. So what would you like to do tonight?"

"What?" In the past five years, Evan had never asked her that question. He commanded and she complied.

"It's a special night tonight," he said, "and I thought you might want to have dinner or go out or something."

"And not fuck?"

"Jesus, woman! Ever since we've been together that's all we've done. Do you realize we've never actually had a reasonable conversation that didn't have to do with sex? You've never once expressed an interest in me or my work or anything else outside of my bedroom."

"Oh. I didn't think it mattered."

Evan crossed the room and took her hand, bringing it to his lips. "It matters, Magda. Quite honestly, you have been the most important person in my life. And tonight, after our celebration, I will tell you why and how." He pulled her out of bed and embraced her, his semierect penis snuggling into her stomach. Then he pushed her away and slapped her naked ass. "Now get dressed, vixen, and get the hell out of here so I can get some work done."

Magda did not spend most of the day sleeping, as was her wont. Instead she simply lay still, hands clasped together on her abdomen, eyes closed, wondering about what Evan had said. She knew something of his life, after five years how could she not? Evan was a gifted doctor, a geneticist by specialty and a brilliant man by all reports. But the content and body of his work meant nothing to her; he could have been a truck driver or a short-order cook. The career he chose was irrelevant to their relationship.

In fact, until he spoke earlier, she'd never even considered that what they had was a relationship. As a single-minded creature of instinct, Magda's interests were basic. Shelter, sustenance and sex. And not necessarily in that particular order. She provided the first two for herself and the third was given by others for as long as they continued to please her.

She rose and began to prepare herself for the evening, fervently hoping Evan was not planning some demonstration of his affections. A marriage proposal would be a death knell, even a declaration of love could be a disaster.

When he greeted her at his door with a kiss, her worst fears were confirmed. And when he presented her with a single white rose and the words "For you, my love," every instinct within her urged her to turn and run, or stand and fight. Instead she allowed him to put an arm around her and seat her on the couch.

"Comfortable?" Evan poured a glass of deep red wine and offered it to her.

"Evan," she began, "you know I don't drink—"

"I know, Magda. I do indeed know. But tonight," he said, handing her the glass, "tonight you will drink."

Her eyes darted from his face to the wine and back to his face again.

"It will be fine, trust me." Evan gave a sharp chuckle. "Trust the doctor."

First love and now trust? Magda held her glass up and studied the color of the wine. Such a beautiful poison, she thought and realized she would drink. Simply because he'd asked. Five years of what she had thought was mock submission to this man had become real. She was his to command.

Evan stared at her, as if reading her mind. A slow, sinister smile moved over his lips. "Drink."

Magda drank, sipping slowly at first, gagging on the bitterness and death the wine held for her, choking on the self-hatred her obedience contained.

"All of it."

She sipped again. The second taste was not as bad as the first; like the abandoning of pride, the task became easier with each swallow. Finally she drained it completely,

"Good girl."

She tried to place the empty glass on the table in front of her, but her hand shook. The crystal fell to the floor and shattered, leaving one small drop of wine on the carpet. She looked up from the floor to his face. "Evan?" Magda's voice sounded faint even to her own ears.

"Yes, I'm sure you feel a bit dizzy right now. Sit still, close your eyes and allow the drug to work. It's painless, my dear. Maybe even pleasurable, if you will abandon yourself to it. And as you drop away, I will tell you my story."

The wine burned through her veins, her stomach rolled, she felt the beat of her heart slow with each passing second. Even without the drug, Magda knew she had no choice but to obey. She rested her head on the back of the couch and listened to voice of her master, Evan.

"I knew who and what you were long before we met. I had been watching for signs of one of your kind and when I found you I knew I had to keep you near me, long enough to study you and to commence and complete my work. But what could I offer to a creature like you, one blessed with eternal life and beauty and youth? One possessing more power than any mortal, man or woman?"

Magda looked up at him, suddenly knowing the answer, and he laughed cruelly at the realization in her eyes.

"I certainly had no intention of giving you either my blood or my life. So I gave you what you could never have. An absolute surrender. And oh, Magda, you are so good at that surrender, it is almost a shame our time is coming to an end."

Magda's mind reeled with the possibility of her own death. It was something she'd never before considered. She was an immortal creature, or so she'd thought until this moment. The fact that she could be wrong, was wrong, chilled the already sluggish flow of blood in her veins. Her eyes narrowed and her lips pulled tight in a grimace of anger.

Evan laughed. "Don't scowl at me, Magda. You wouldn't want to ruin your porcelain white skin with wrinkles, would you? Resistance will do you no good anyway, and neither will a display of temper. Bow your head, my dear, and accept the inevitable."

She had no intention of doing either. Instead she swallowed hard and brought one harsh word up out of her throat. "Why?"

He smiled at her, an indulgent smile one might give to an inferior; she seethed with rage at his condescension, but he continued. "It has long been my theory that the female vampire might be an interesting creature to study. Given the fact that they don't age, caught and trapped at the peak of their sexual potency, I surmised it was a possibility that their reproductive organs might still function. And thanks to my experiments on you, I proved my theory correct."

She glanced down at the floor and the broken glass. If I could move, she thought, I could cut his throat with that.

"Pay attention to me." He leaned over, slapped her face, then grasped her chin, tilting her head up. "You, my dear, are a depository of fertilized ova, all of them potential creatures of death and destruction like yourself, but frozen at the moment of conception, kept ageless and preserved by the vampire genes which are your legacy. How long have you lived? Five centuries? Eight?"

Magda shook her head. "Longer," she whispered. He'd taken his hands from her and her eyes dropped back to the floor, studying the shards of crystal. That piece, there, she thought with a touch of triumph, I could use that one.

"It doesn't matter, really." Evan shrugged off her comment. "What matters is that many of your sexual encounters resulted in cells that had the potential of life. I have been harvesting these cells, experimenting with different sorts of environments in which they can grow, in which they can properly gestate."

Magda shifted her body forward on the sofa slightly.

"Perhaps you want to know whether I succeeded? But of course you do. And I'm happy to say I have. And so it turns out congratulations are in order. For both of us." He laughed again. "You are mother, Magda, to twenty magnificent creatures like yourself. Pity you won't live long enough to enjoy maternity."

He took his eyes away from her and looked back over his shoulder, to where two white-coated men entered the room. Evan nodded to them. "She's ready now, gentlemen. Shall we finish the job?"

She lurched off the couch in a desperate attempt to escape but the muscles in her legs seemed paralyzed by the drug. Landing in a tangle of limbs on top of the broken glass, she gasped with pain, her fingers fumbling to pick up one of the shards, but failing to grasp it. Then she faded away into the familiar dream which, she now knew, was not a dream.

Hands grasped her roughly, and carried her to that cold place, stripping her clothing from her body and laying her on a cold steel surface. Her wrists and ankles were fastened with metal cuffs, the smell of the air was rich with fear and disinfectant and then blood. Her blood. Her eyes shot open as the sharp stroke of a scalpel opened her from breasts to groin.

"She's awake," one of the men said. She rolled her eyes to the side to see him and he backed away. "She knows what we're doing."

"And your point is?" Evan's voice sounded faraway.

"It's inhumane," the other man stuttered, "it's, it's, well, it's horrible. She must be in a great deal of pain."

"She's not human." Evan said, coming nearer. "So your point is again?"

"Nothing, Dr. Thomas."

"Good," he said. Magda felt his hands probe around inside her. "There," the hands moved away and Evan's voice was triumphant now, with a frightening note of finality, "that's the last of them. Leave her for now; we'll do the last dose of drugs when we're done with this last egg."

"But shouldn't we close the incision? And what if the drug wears off more? She's already more awake than she should be."

"Didn't you hear me?" Evan lowered his voice to a threatening depth. "I said, leave her."

"Yes, sir."

Magda lay still, listening to the sounds of the men moving away. She heard a door shut, and looked around at the room. Good, she thought, no windows, so no one will be watching. Evan should have listened to his assistant, the drug was wearing off; he may have known a lot about her, but he didn't know it all, had no comprehension of her limits, her ability to regenerate, her very strong desire to survive. Her mouth curved into a triumphant smile.

She tried moving her hands within their restraints and was rewarded with a slight loosening. Again and again, she pulled until finally one of the metal cuffs broke apart, followed quickly by the other. She sat up, feeling the warmth of blood washing over her stomach.

Magda grimaced in pain, pulled the flaps of her skin together as if she were closing a garment and waited for the pain to subside. When she finally felt the healing begin, she reached down to pull off the restraints on her ankles, grinning when the metal shattered in her grip.

Swinging her legs around, she picked up the scalpel left on the small table next to her and slid silently to her feet.

She swayed for a moment and steadied herself on the operating table, then began walking to the door through which Evan and the men had left. Her steps were slow and staggering, but by the time she reached the door, she had recovered some of her strength.

"More than enough," Magda whispered as she put a hand to the doorknob, "more than enough to deal with human males."

The door opened quietly and Magda entered. The room was warm and she inhaled deeply, pulling the heat into her lungs, feeling her body rejuvenate with each new breath. Row upon row of glass coffin-shaped tanks filled the room. Some were empty but others contained a red liquid in which human forms writhed and twisted. Two men hovered over one of the tanks and she approached them, scalpel in hand.

Silently, she drove the blade below the right ear of the closest man, cutting deeply and curving around to end up at his left ear. He slumped over, his upper body dropping into the tank, his blood pouring out, darkening the liquid within. The other man, the compassionate one who dared to argue with Evan about her, stared at his dead associate for a second, watched as clawed hands reached up and pulled the man deeper into the tank. Then his eyes traveled from that sight to Magda, standing naked and angry in front of him. Like countless others before him, he was mesmerized and enraptured by the sight of her flawless body. She felt his shock as he stared at the healed incision on her stomach. His lips moved soundlessly and he began to tremble.

She smiled at him and clasped him in her arms. "Because of your kindness," she whispered, "your death will be enjoyable. For both of us." Her mouth fastened on his neck and she drew his blood into her mouth, draining him completely and rejuvenating her weakened body.

And now for Evan.

There was a door on the opposite wall and she moved toward it, stopping at all the occupied tanks on the way, to twist the neck of each poor creature within. The killing grew more difficult for Magda with each successive form; they were all male and they all wore the faces of former lovers, but they were weak and helpless and there was no doubt in her mind that they must die as their fathers had before them. None would remain to walk the earth.

After disposing of the last body, she reached the door, wiping the slick red liquid that now coated her hands onto the walls. Magda tightened her grip on the scalpel and turned back to survey the room, making a quick count. "Nineteen. But he said twenty," she whispered, "where is the final one?"

The answer awaited her on the opening of the door. Two identical men stood there, both of them clothed in garments she knew were Evan's. The one facing her glanced up at her entrance, shook his head slightly and turned his attention back to the other. The real Evan was explaining the cloning process to his double, pointing out the notebooks lined up along one wall, which, he said, detailed all his research. "Don't forget, though, that you are the best of them," Evan said. "I've embedded my knowledge and memories in you. You're my son and the inheritor of all I have."

Evan must have missed the twisted smile appearing on the face of the man he instructed. He even missed the gleam of anticipation in that duplicate pair of eyes as Magda approached soundlessly. She held back a laugh. Evan was a fool after all. Brilliant, true, and capable of doing great things. He had accomplished what she had never thought was possible; the attempts she'd made to replicate beings like herself had always failed. Yet after all that, he was still a fool. This creature was not his son, but hers. Her endowment to him, the blood lust, was written plainly on his body; Evan should have been able to read the clues. But, poor dear, she thought, he's only human. *And now he's a dead human.*

She drove the scalpel into his back, twisting the blade, appreciating the glorious burst of blood staining the back of his white lab coat. He gasped and turned to look at her, his eyes filled with pain and confusion. She smiled, kissed his cheek and gave him a push, into the waiting arms and teeth of their son.

When it was over, he looked up at her, gleeful and glowing with his first meal, his mouth coated with Evan's blood. "Mother?" The body dropped to the floor.

She shook her head, walked over to him and licked the blood from his lips. "Call me Magda. I am and will be much more than a mother to you. And I will call you Evan." She gestured to the notebooks on the shelves and kicked the body lying bloodless at her feet. "Do you understand how he did this?"

He nodded.

"And do you indeed hold his knowledge and his memories?"

She held her breath for a minute. So much depended on his answer, this man with the face and eyes so like Evan's.

"Every bit of him," he said, reaching out and caressing her naked breasts. Then he grinned and it was as if she were looking into a mirror. He had her smile, her teeth, her fangs. "Except I am better than he. Finally, you have the perfect lover." His face darkened a bit with that thought. "But who will give me the bliss of surrender?"

Magda threw her head back and laughed. Perfect indeed, an ideal blend of Evan and herself. Suddenly the centuries didn't seem as long. "Don't worry, darling," she took him by the arm and led him back through the lab into Evan's apartment. "We'll take turns."

THE MIRRORED IMAGE

Her name is Lizzie Clayton; thin, with long black hair and pale skin, she is unremarkable. The man is nameless, an anonymous suited body that blends with all the others. They are alone in a room containing one very large table and many chairs. He sits on one of the chairs, padded in black leather with chrome legs and wheels.

She kneels in front of him and unzips his pants, working them over his buttocks and dropping them down around his ankles. She looks up at him from where she kneels, her eyes, smoky grey and questioning. He nods and her tiny hands work at removing his underwear. Soon he is naked from waist to ankles, the nudity looking oddly incongruous with his dressed torso and feet. But she does not see the humor, she is rubbing his penis with her hands, working it delicately up and down, until it jerks and hardens in response. He glances over his shoulder to their reflection in the windowed wall, then turns his chair slightly so that he can have a better view.

Lizzie's tongue darts out between her small white teeth. Still stroking him with one hand, she reaches into the pocket of her skirt and removes a small package. "It's a shame to cover it up," she says, her voice raspy and hoarse. It is something she always says, knowing that they both want the protection. She tears the package open and rolls the condom onto his erect penis. The scent of strawberry fills the air, sweet, cloying and slightly nauseating.

She gives a calculated moan and her mouth goes down to cover him. It is hard to believe that such a small mouth could hold his penis, but she takes it in entirely. He puts his hands down on her head, and watches her suck him in the glass of the window, thinking, perhaps, of other people watching him, watching her. But there is no one to see.

Lizzie's head bobs up and down on his lap, sucking, teasing him with her tongue and teeth. His breath deepens and he groans, pulling her head away from him. She knows what this means and, lifting her skirt, she spins around and presents her bare behind to his gaze. With a sputtering breath, he throws himself off the chair, and kneels behind her. His hands explore the white, naked skin of her buttocks. His tongue runs over his lips quickly, frantically, and he grasps her hips tightly, plunging deeply into her.

She is warm, welcoming and the air becomes thick with the smell of strawberries and sex. His hands reach and burrow their way under her thin cotton blouse, grabbing at her breasts. He twists her nipples in his fingers, still thrusting in and out of her, over and over. She makes encouraging noises, noises that could mean yes, that could mean more. "Yes," he says and "more," he says and suddenly he begins the wheezing moans that signify his orgasm.

And as he is coming, time stops for Lizzie. She feels a coldness deep within her and the voice that has only lately haunted her begins. It is a soft, insistent voice, whispery and spiderlike. It talks of things that even Lizzie does not know, hidden delights and sins, forbidden tastes and touches. It scares her. It thrills her to her very soul.

"Blood," it urges. "Give me blood."

Finally, the man comes, totally unnoticed by Lizzie. The pulse that pounds in her head drowns out the man's loud, pleasured groans, and deadens the sensation of his spurting orgasm.

All she can hear is the voice. All she can feel is the hunger.

"Blood," the voice cries, "give me life and give me blood."

When the man finishes and withdraws, he seems shy, embarrassed. Lizzie smoothes her skirt back down over her slim hips and gives him a warm smile. "Thank you," she kisses his cheek gently, "that was very nice."

Still naked from the waist down the man blushes slightly and reaches into his suit coat pocket. He pulls out his wallet and removes two crisp bills, hundreds. "You were wonderful," he says, handing her the money, then hurriedly turns away to dress himself. The door opens. "I'll call you."

"Good night." Lizzie crumples the money into her pocket, and pushes the button for the elevator. Now, at last, she could go home and get some sleep.

I enjoy myself when Lizzie sleeps. I am free to think, then, free to remember. She doesn't know where her dreams come from, doesn't attempt to analyze the strange thoughts that have possessed her for some time. Self-analysis is not one of her strong points and the thoughts, quite frankly, are not hers but mine. As for me, I don't quite know what I am now. I was once a woman, very much like her in physical appearance. After I ceased to be a woman, I became one of the undead. And after I ceased to be undead, I was, well, just there, or better perhaps, just here. It's a long story but we have the time; Lizzie should sleep well for a while.

Wulfstan joined our campfire one evening, just as our meal was finished. Dark-complected and swathed in a black cloak, he flashed a white grin at us and mentioned an acquaintance in another camp, by way of introduction. At his telling of his name, a few of the older women crossed themselves, muttering a prayer to the Holy Virgin, and a few of the old men grumbled slightly, but my father made the traditional welcome. Wulfstan bowed and accepted a place in the circle, allaying most fears by accepting a drink of the sweet, red wine that we loved. When Sophie made her test of him, bringing the heavy silver crucifix she wore into seemingly accidental contact with the bare skin of his hand, he showed no reaction other than a warm smile for her and my people were satisfied.

For me, you understand, it would have made no difference if he were nosferatu; he could even have been Satan himself. I was his from the moment I saw him, whether he chose to claim me or not. I was utterly captivated by him, so different from the boys I knew, so different from the men who looked at me with a knowing eye.

It was inevitable, I suppose. I was only thirteen when he first came among us; the touch of his eyes over my yet virginal body created strange longings in me. I could see no other man than him, would accept no other suitors. My father, I know, despaired that I would forever be unwed. But since I was his only child and companion, my mother having been dead for many years, he kept me with him, not forcing me into marriage.

Wulfstan only came to us a few nights a year, but he was always welcomed as a returning son. The lengthy periods between his visits had become commonplace and were eventually used jokingly to measure time. "When will that stubborn hen begin laying again?" would come the question and the inevitable answer would be, "when Wulfstan returns." And at the mention of his name, I would shudder and writhe at the fire that rushed through my veins, but I said nothing, keeping my dark longings to myself.

Then one night, two months after my sixteenth birthday, he appeared, only days after his last visit. He singled out my father from the circle and pulled him aside. I strained to hear their words, but they were too far away. Then my father turned around, his great booming laugh echoing off the shadowy trees. "Wulfstan," he clapped him on the shoulder, "has returned to us tonight to take a wife."

My heart fell within me, it must be Marie, I thought, she trembled when she touched his hand over a cup of wine on his last visit. Or Giselle, perhaps, who shared a kiss with him before he left a year ago. Or any one of many girls who had sighed over his face, his curly black hair, his silvery grey eyes. I had never felt such despair and stared down at the dirt at my feet, my long dark hair hanging like a curtain in front of my face.

Then a pair of shining leather boots stood in front of me and two strong pale hands reached down for mine. "Lizbeth," he pulled me to my feet and his voice seemed to speak deep inside my mind, "I choose you, if you will have me."

Still I would not raise my eyes to look at him. I could not. But he took my chin in his hand, pulling my head up. When our eyes locked together, he smiled for me, only for me, and I knew him for what he was. Knew it without fear, for his eyes spoke not of death, not of pain, but of passion and desire and eternal pleasure.

We were wed that night, so many centuries ago. Before the full moon had even climbed to mid-sky, we were sealed and I had packed up my belongings. His wagon was not far, he said, and he wanted to take me back to his camp to meet his mother. The old women sighed their approval and the young girls shed a few tears at their loss of him. My father gave me a warm hug and a whispered blessing. And Wulfstan took my hand and led me away through the night forest.

His wagon was far enough away that I began to grow tired of the walk and my feet began to falter on the dark paths. He sensed my weakness and swept me up into his arms. I believe I must have slept for when he finally set me down outside his wagon, the moon had traveled beyond our sight. "We will stay here for the day," he said, looking down at me, "I prefer to travel at night." I nodded my understanding, unable to control a slight shiver, and he gave a low laugh. "Ah, Lizbeth, my little lamb, you don't need to fear me. I will not hurt you."

"Wulfstan," it was the first time I had ever said his name aloud, after three years of whispering it to my soul. I savored its sweetness on my tongue, "I am yours to do with as you wish."

He said nothing, but smiled and we entered his wagon. When he lit a lantern I could see that it was strangely yet beautifully finished inside. Black silk draped the walls, black fur covered the floor. There was no cot to sleep on, but pillows were piled together, almost disguising the rectangular box in one corner. He lifted an eyebrow at me for my reaction. With trembling fingers, I loosened the tie that held my dress fastened and slid the garment over my shoulders, gathering the material at my waist, while exposing my naked breasts to his intent gaze.

Slowly, as if time and all the world were suspended between us, he crossed the wagon and reached his hand out to me. His touch was like that of a torch, setting my skin on fire where it came too close.

He lowered me to the floor and tore the gathered dress from my unresisting hands and body. Then he began to remove his own clothing. His skin was pale, almost white, but his chest and shoulders were covered with thick, black hair as was the place where his penis rose, magnificently, proudly. I was a virgin, but not totally unused to the male organ. I had, after all, seen the range of sizes from male babies to the herd stallion, had done some mutual exploration with boys of my own age. I'd even gotten a glimpse of Demetri's erection one evening before he closed the curtain of his wagon. But Demetri's wife, it seemed, had been cheated, and as Wulfstan's penis grew, I began to believe that so had the mares.

My hands reached out of their own accord to stroke him and he gave a low moan. "I will try to be gentle," he assured me, "but there will be some pain." He kissed me, delicately at first, concentrating on my lips and face, moving eventually to my neck and my breasts. When his teeth clenched upon my nipple, I gasped, not in pain, but at the wildness that consumed my body. His cold, long fingers found me and entered, probing and thrusting, testing the resistance of my barrier. I felt a sharp pang, as if something had been torn away within me.

When Wulfstan pulled his fingers away, his nails were extended and sharp and covered with blood. He smiled and licked at them, then put his head between my legs to lap up the rest of the blood that had been spilt. I put my hands on top of his head, holding him there, wondering at this sucking of me, the licking and thrusting of his tongue. The pain disappeared as suddenly as it came and was replaced by the feel of his mouth, his hands molding me, and his silky hair tangling around my fingers.

And still his mouth continued to work on me until the building tension was more than I could bear. His tongue touching, his breath warming, his fingers probing, every sensation was distinct and clear. An inarticulate scream rose from deep within me, found its way to my throat and I writhed and shivered in an ecstasy I wanted never to end.

Then Wulfstan lifted his mouth from me, scenting the air as I had seen wolves in the forest do, when on the trail of their prey. I almost expected him to throw his head back and howl in passion and hunger. I didn't matter; I had no fear of him, although I knew my death could be in that cry. I wanted to hear him howl, wanted my last earthly gaze to be his face splattered with my heart's blood. I wanted him to devour me, body and soul. Instead, he looked at me and gave a low laugh, his silver eyes glowing eerily in the lantern's flame. Slowly, languorously, he crawled up the length of my body. The touch of his naked skin brushing against mine caused me to shudder again and again. When our faces were together, he exposed his teeth to me. They were sharp, glistening.

I reached a trembling hand out and touched his cheek. "Wulfstan." I breathed his name as if in prayer, for to me, at that moment, he was a god. My god, the only being I would ever worship. And if that worship entailed the offering of my life, it was well given.

He read the thoughts in my mind. "No, Lizbeth, it is not your death I seek. I will make you my mate in eternal life, for you have a soul like mine, an appetite like mine. And after I awaken you, we shall live forever."

Wulfstan paused, not laying on me, but holding himself delicately balanced above me, so close that I felt the touch of his body hair on my skin. He was waiting for something, some action on my part, acquiescence, perhaps or invitation. I could not speak the words, instead, I arched my body up to meet his. With a low throaty growl, he clasped his arms around me and plunged deeply into me. The sound that escaped my lips was as close to a howl as was humanly possible and Wulfstan laughed before his mouth came down to silence my cries. "You see," he said between kisses, "a soul like mine."

He was insatiable. Again and again he thrust into me, his penis as hard as granite, filling me, reaching to the very center of my being and beyond. I writhed and shuddered under his every touch, never wanting it to end.

Just before dawn, Wulfstan stopped and withdrew, growing quiet on top of me, with only the pulsing of his penis against my groin to remind me of our passion. "Not much time left to us, my lamb. May I feed?"

At my nod, his eyes glowed, their light making the lantern dim. He opened his mouth, exposing again his sharpened, white canines. His teeth came down on my neck, puncturing the skin and as he began to draw my blood into him, he entered me again. The feeling of blood being pulled from me into him, along with the forceful thrusts of his penis, and the rapid explosion of his climax, caused my head to swim and I reached orgasm once again. Time stopped.

When my eyes fluttered open again, Wulfstan was standing over me, tying his tunic with his long, pale fingers. He reached down to me and drew me up, holding me tightly against his chest. "I must sleep," he whispered. "But you are safe here for the day. You, too, must rest." His laugh caused the hair on my neck to raise. "You will need it come tomorrow night." He kissed me and crawled into his box, pulling the lid closed. I piled the pillows on the floor, and slept next to him, curling up my naked body closely to his coffin, embracing the wood as if it were his flesh.

These are the dreams that Lizzie dreams; the ones she can't explain, the ones that make her wake with dry mouth and body aching for something she can't define. I know what it is she desires, but I am trapped here inside her, until the day that she awakens.

Through her eyes, though, I can watch as she prepares herself for the day. She always starts with a shower, and the tingling feel of sharp razor against legs, armpits and pubic area, then the douche, with its medicinal fragrance and flowing coolness. She lingers over this longer than normal, aroused perhaps by the remembered fragments of her dreams. Her fingers go unerringly to the stiffening clitoris and begin stroking, palpating. Her nipples harden, she rubs them up against the mirrored shower wall. With one hand she rhythmically moves the nozzle in and out, the other continues to circle and tease.

Lizzie closes her eyes, thinking of nothing but the sensations she is causing, the warmth of her vagina, the heat of her fingers, the tautness of her breasts. Then the sharp, quick force of her orgasm shocks her, causing her to cry out. She stands for a while, shuddering as the hot water of the shower washes over her body. She gives a girlish giggle, looks into the misty mirror and with a smile, leans over to kiss her reflection. Her tongue darts quickly over the smooth surface as if to find her lover's mouth and she laughs. "Morning, Lizbeth," she says, puzzling only for a second over the choice of the name, and steps out of the shower.

After dressing, she consults her calendar. An easy day, she nods to herself, only three jobs, two of them repeats. She mentally ticks each one off—the first one over by nine, the second done by eleven and the new one not scheduled until nine that evening. She smiles as she puts on her coat, and goes out the door, a whole afternoon with nothing to do, what luxury.

Her first trick of the day is an oral surgeon she'd met once when having a root canal. He's kinky, she thinks, but not the way one would imagine. Such a gentle man with gentle hands and all she needs to do is sit on the floor by him where he lies fully reclined in the dental chair, and hold his hand while he talks, not about sex, but about how much he dislikes his job, his wife, his life. Even at that, his talk is not vehement or malicious, only the sad, bittersweet disillusionment of age. Lizzie judges him to be in his mid-sixties and especially likes the look of his eyes when he removes his glasses. They are small and slightly crinkled up at the edges as if he could have been a mirthful man had life given him the opportunity.

When his talk finally winds down, she is only required to do one more thing. She lays her head on his chest so that he can touch her hair and she grasps his stubby penis in gloved hands, manipulating him slowly. It does not take him long to come, an amazingly copious spurt of semen erupts after just a few strokes. She knows that he has been fondling himself while he talked, although she keeps that secret for him, like all of his others. After he is done, she wipes up his spend with one of the office paper towels, delicately reinserts his penis into his pants and zips him back up. The entire process takes no more than half an hour and Lizzie always feels guilty taking his money, five hundred this time. She'd do it for nothing, simply because he's a sad, old man who seems to need her. But it would offend him, so she thanks him, slipping the money into her purse. He kisses her forehead before she leaves. "Good day, my dear," he says as if he had just cleaned her teeth, "and don't forget to floss."

The second trick proves to be more interesting, and much livelier. He is a large, burly man, more like a bear than a wolf, but animal enough for my liking. He is waiting for her at the hotel room that she rents on occasion. Unlike the dentist, he doesn't want to talk, has no interest in relating any details of his life. It is quite clear that he is there for only one thing, and he wastes no time in small talk or preliminaries. Almost before she can lock the door, he comes to her, rapidly removing his clothes. Once he is completely naked, he quickly undresses her and tosses all the clothes in the corner of the room.

His hands are demanding and they press against her flesh relentlessly. He is already wearing a condom, he always does, apparently not wanting to take the time with it once she arrives. She has never seen him without an erection, even after they have sex he remains rock hard. She wonders, as his mouth travels the length of her body, if he ever has any other woman besides her. He is always so frantic for her, so desperate, that she thinks he must not.

He cups his calloused hands under the bottom of her breasts, and bends down to suckle each nipple, flattening her up against the door in his urgency. His erect penis burns into her stomach and he grinds it into her. Then he reaches down, grasps her buttocks and pulls her up to him. She wraps her legs around his waist and he shifts her position only slightly before ramming his full length into her. He grunts and groans, pushing into her again and again. Lizzie twines her arms around his neck and holds him to her, suppressing a giggle, not at him, but at the thought that his frenzy might bring the door down and they'd end up rolling down the hallway. She doubts that it would break his concentration.

Her smile only lasts for a second. With a start, she realizes that she has begun to respond to him. It has never happened before—at least not with clients. She has always worked hard to retain her professional outlook. But now she feels her pulse rise and her body answer to his passion. He falters a bit, sensing the difference in her, then shakes his head and continues.

With each stroke of him inside her, Lizzie becomes more aroused. A new world opens before her and her senses expand. The rough texture of the wood on her back is exciting; the brush of his chest against hers, the hands tightly grasping, his heavy breathing in her hair, everything has acquired a new dimension. And she senses the odors around her, the starchy smell of the freshly-made bed, his musky male scent, the sweat and the semen. And his blood. Oh, God, she moans, his blood.

At that thought, her mind unfolds, opening itself more widely to my invasion. "The blood, Lizzie," I urge, "take the blood. Give us the blood."

The idea takes hold, her eyes roll back into her head and she begins to chant the word in time with the man's thrusts. "Blood," she says as he pushes into her, "Blood." At first the word is whispered, not audible above the sounds of their sex. But it grows louder with each new stroke, until even he can hear. "Blood. Blood. Blood." Her teeth close around his neck and she bites.

"Jesus," he pulls away from her so fast that she falls to the floor with a thud. Her eyes return to normal and she looks at him in shock.

"What's wrong, baby?" she asks, soothingly. "Why did you stop?"

Looking down at her in disgust, he says nothing but goes to the corner, picks up her clothes and throws them at her. "Get dressed," he snarls, "I don't never want to see you again."

She fumbles with her clothes and he removes his wallet from the dresser. "I guess I'll have to pay you, anyway, won't I?" He tosses one bill down to her. "That's short 'cause I didn't get to finish, bitch. But I warned you when we first started that I didn't like that kinky stuff—all I wanted was just a straight fuck every now and then."

"But," Lizzie begins, then thinks better of it. She can't remember what happened so she can't really explain. Pulling herself up from the floor, she rubs her sore bottom and stares at the money in her hand with distaste. "Here," she says and drops the bill to the floor, "you can get someone else. Leave the key at the desk." She walks out, slamming the door behind her.

Although her mind is not analytical, Lizzie puzzles over his, and her own, strange behavior as she walks to her apartment. Her sexual response surprises her, he had been one of her regulars for over a year and nothing like that had ever occurred before. And she never blacks out, never faints. Oh, well, she shrugs as she opens her front door, there's always a first time, I guess.

She flops down on her couch, picks up her remote control and turns on the TV and VCR. Lately she's become addicted to the mysterious happenings shows, the ones that discuss UFO sightings and abductions, ghosts and other supernatural occurrences. The one she taped last night has to do with vampires, a subject that doesn't particularly interest her. She watches for a while, seeing so-called scientists examine and display the bones of supposed vampires in different areas around the world. She yawns and checks the clock. It's only eleven-thirty, she has plenty of time, and she stretches out on the sofa and sleeps.

Wulfstan and I lived a nomadic, yet idyllic, existence for the next five years. Periodically, he would leave me at the wagon and go off for an hour or so. I knew he went to feed, but asked no questions.

Then one night, after we had made love, he looked me deep in the eyes. "Lizbeth," he said, his low voice never failing to give me shivers, "it will soon be time for you to make your choice."

"Choice," my voice faltered, "what do you mean?"

"I can awaken you to my existence, so that you would be like me eternally. Or you can leave me, to find a normal life in the mortal world."

"Leave you?" In the five years since we had been wed, that thought had never once crossed my mind. The very hint of it made me want to weep. Leave Wulfstan? "I'd rather die." I hadn't meant to say the words aloud.

A grim smile darkened his face. "The transformation is often dangerous, and once accomplished, it can never be undone. You would bear no children, never know the joys of a natural existence. You would have to shun the sun, have to take the lives of humans to continue your own. It means, my little lamb, you would become one with the wolf and the birds of prey. And although I want to keep you with me forever, I will not force the choice on you. Your decision must be freely given and with love."

He got up from our bed of pillows and pulled on his chausses, looking down on me with silvered eyes. "You have taken my seed for five years now, that will aid the transformation, perhaps even over time, cause it. But if you left now, the traces of me would eventually fade away, allowing you to live normally, grow old, die and acquire your final salvation. I can offer nothing but damnation." I had never heard his voice so humble, so contrite. "Damnation, Lizbeth, and my love."

"Then, Wulfstan, I choose your love. I care nothing for damnation."

"Good." I could tell that he was satisfied with my answer, satisfied that I knew what he offered and choose it willingly.

He knelt back down on the pillows. "Little lamb, this will hurt, much more than the separation of your maidenhead the first time we made love." His eyes began to glow. "Ah, what a night that was. It will live with me forever."

I smiled up at him and nodded.

"I must drain most of your blood," he explained, "then replace it with some of my own. I cannot give you enough to completely replenish you, but tomorrow night, after our rest, we will feed."

"I am not afraid, Wulfstan. Do what you must."

Suddenly he fell on me and his teeth ripped and slashed the skin on my neck. In an instinctual attempt to avoid the pain I tried to move away, but his strong hands held my shoulders pinioned to the floor. I was unprepared for the savageness of his attack, even in his most passionate moments he had always been gentle with me. But this was not love, I realized, relaxing slightly as the blood flowed from me into him, it was survival. A great blackness began to wash over me as he drank, suckling at my neck, but I forgave him the pain, wanting only to share myself with him forever.

And when I felt the cold drawing of death upon me, like a great wave, the taste of him and his blood blossomed in my mouth. My eyes opening wide, but unseeing, I drank in the essence of him, frantically swallowing him, as I had often drunk of his seed. But the revelations of him were greater than any sensation I had ever experienced. I was making love to his very soul and once joined we would never be parted, but together forever in a sensuality and unity that made sex seem inadequate, unnecessary.

It was over too soon, as all good things are, and he pried my mouth away from his wrist. "Enough, Lizbeth, you will weaken me too much." And he laughed to let me know that he was pleased. Then he picked me up, carried me to his coffin and pulled the lid over the two of us. I slept and when I woke it was to a new world, a new life.

The life following my transformation was not as idyllic as the years before. Plague had struck the land and healthy victims were difficult to find. Now that there were two of us to feed—we required

all the blood from an adult human at least once each cycle of the
moon—our tracks were more difficult to hide. For hide we must,
Wulfstan told me, or we would be killed. And he explained to me the
ways we could die: a stake through the heart, exposure to the sun,
burning at the stake, decapitation. But he also taught to me the
wonders of our lives: how to read the stars, to scent the night air and
count the numbers and types of wildlife near, how to lure prey, human
or animal, into our grasps. We would take animal blood on occasion,
if the human type was inaccessible, but it never seemed enough.

Slowly we traveled the length of our country and entered the next.
Wulfstan's ancestral home was not far from the border and when we
reached it we would be safe. There lived the survivors of our kind,
family and kin I had never met, and there also were servants to protect
and conceal us, mortals who had served in his family for generation
upon generation. Although Wulfstan had used the word, I knew that
he did not mean a family as I had known; there would be no babies,
no children, no old men or women. Most were related only by blood
and lives entwined.

Wulfstan had spent many centuries searching for other vampires,
building up his home into a sort of fortress, a safe harbor for the
creatures of the night. He mentioned their names to me as we climbed
the hill that overlooked his land. "Celia," he said with a smile and a
shake of his head, "you'll like her I think, not much older than you in
body, she's been with us for 150 years. And Griegg, of course, and
Pieter...." I had never seen Wulfstan so elated, his face was lit with
longing for his friends. I took his arm in mine and hugged him close
to me.

He looked down at me with an indulgent smile, "Soon, Lizbeth,
my lamb, we'll be home." Then he stopped suddenly and lifted his

head, scenting the air. Suddenly, his expression changed from joy to rage.

"Wulfstan?" I whispered his name in alarm as he pulled up the horses and swiftly jumped down.

"Stay here," he ordered, his voice harsh and imperious. "And if I don't return, take the wagon and go. Hide. Remember what I have taught you."

"Wulfstan," I called to him as he ran. He did not look back, but crested the hill and disappeared from my sight. I sat in the wagon for a minute, stunned at his sudden change. Then I got down, and slowly, cautiously, walked up the hill.

Wulfstan's fortress was carved into the surrounding hills and guarded by heavy stone walls. Figures were dancing crazily in the courtyard, the windows glowed red and I could see red flames within. At first I thought I must be witnessing a celebration, a ritual.

But as I looked closer I realized that the flames were not hearth fires nor torches, but a wild fire, fed out of control. As my vision continued to sharpen, I saw that this was not a dance but a battle, a massacre. And into this mêlée I saw Wulfstan descend.

"No," I cried as loud as I could, but my words were whipped away by the wind that carried the screams of the courtyard to me.

"Kill the monsters."

"Cut off their heads."

"Burn the bodies."

"Wipe the land free of their demon blood."

Unable to control my fear for Wulfstan's safety, I ran down the hill and paused outside the gates, staring in shock. A young girl, no older than me, was dragged from the burning fortress by her hair and as I watched three men held her down and cut her head from her body.

"Celia." I heard Wulfstan's choked cry in my head.

"Here," the leader of the marauders called, "here is the devil lord, himself. At him, men."

Ten of the men, armed with heavy swords and cudgels, began to encircle Wulfstan. He fought bravely, ripping the throat out of three of them before they even knew he was near. But there were too many, even for him and two men crept up behind him, bludgeoning his head again and again, until his head exploded into bright blood. His eyes met mine briefly as he fell.

"Run," I heard his whispered voice in my soul. "Hide."

But I could not. And as the leader swept his sword down and severed Wulfstan's head from his body, I howled and flung myself on them. I killed two more of the dogs, with nothing but my nails and my teeth, laughing as their coarse blood flowed down my arms and throat. Of course it was an impossible battle, and as they held me down, I spat at them and gave them my death curse.

"I will return, we will all return, and you shall be our food forever, you and every generation following you."

Then the sword came down and that is all I remember, until one day my spirit seemed to rise up out of that dark place, into the air, free at last. A crowd of people were standing over a pile of charred, blackened bones, studying one particular reconstructed skeleton.

"The whole fortress seemed to have been destroyed," an older man was saying, "and the inhabitants, decapitated, mutilated and burned in a common fire. Some of the bones that were buried deeper in the pile are still in good condition."

"They were all killed? Why was that, Doctor? Does anyone know?"

"The people of the time were extremely superstitious. Given the way the bodies were treated after death, I would assume they were judged to be vampires."

"Vampires? A whole fortress of them?" One of the younger men laughed. "That's pretty far-fetched...."

I did not choose to stay in that place. Instead I drifted, aimlessly searching until finally, after many days or many years, I found a body that resembled mine. It was easy enough to submerse myself into Lizzie Clayton and there wait for her awakening, for the blood to bring me back to life.

Lizzie is intrigued by the last trick. He's not her usual type of client, he is elegantly dressed and extremely handsome with dark hair and grey eyes. She wonders why he called her, this man should never have to pay for a woman. He'd arranged to meet her at an exclusive restaurant and she'd dressed with care.

Hesitating in the lobby, she worries that maybe her white, off-the-shoulder sheath dress exposes too much bare skin, but the glow in his eyes as he seats her opposite him at the table, tells her it is just right. They don't talk much through the meal, she is nervous about using the proper etiquette and he seems content to just follow her movements with his eyes. Finally, when the bill is paid, he gets up, walks around the table and pulls out her chair. His hand grazes her bare shoulder and she stifles a gasp. His touch is hot, like fire, like ice.

He takes her to his hotel room, also very exclusive, very elegant. He locks the door and she gives him a smile. "What would you like?" she asks, surprised to hear excitement in her voice.

"You," he says with a low growl, "body and soul."

"Well," Lizzie laughs, "I don't know about the soul, but the body is yours."

"Ah, but I do." He crosses the room and begins to undress her as if she were a child. He removes her shoes and kisses her toes, then runs his tongue and hands slowly up her thighs, catching the hem of her dress in his long fingers and pulling it up over her head. She is naked except for her white lace panties. He grips her waist in his hands and lifts her off her feet, bringing her mouth to his, and still holding her and kissing her, carries her to the bed.

He sets her down, pushing her gently down to the surface of the bed, covering her neck and breasts with thousands of burning kisses. He lingers over her nipples, teasing them with his tongue and teeth until she groans in passion. He smiles and begins to remove his own clothes carelessly, ripping at them, fighting to get out of them as quickly as possible. And then he is naked.

She gives an involuntary gasp—his body is so flawless, his skin so pale it could be made of porcelain, and his penis is so large, the skin stretched so much that it glistened and shone. He reaches over to remove her panties and at his touch, she shivers over and over.

"I will not hurt you, Lizzie," he says and something about his voice is calming, familiar. She touches his cheek bricfly, as if in a remembered caress. His fingers reach inside her and suddenly her entire body seems to explode. She is responding to this man as she has to no other, her entire life. Wants to have him inside her, pulsing and thrusting, more than she's ever wanted anything.

"Do whatever you want." Lizzie closes her eyes and moans. "I'm yours for the night."

He positions himself over her, "No, you are mine forever."

She opens her eyes with a start. Forever? she thinks, but then he thrusts into her and she can think of nothing else but the union of his penis and her vagina and the hot waves of pleasure that overwhelm her.

He grinds into her and she wraps her legs around his back to hold him in; she never wants to lose this feeling. Her entire body is covered in sweat and he bends down to lick the beads of salt from her breasts. The touch of his tongue sends more shivers through her body and she comes, quickly and violently, screaming incoherently.

He throws his head back and howls, then falls heavily upon her, his mouth on her neck. His teeth are sharp and nip at her skin, but she doesn't care. She is too absorbed in the other sensations he is causing. The sharp pinch of pain only adds to her arousal and she grabs his head, holding his mouth to her, not feeling or caring that her life is slowly, surely, being drawn from her.

Then he comes and the force of his orgasm seems to drive her away from him. She feels the sticky warmth of his semen fill her vagina, overflowing onto her thighs and onto the top of the bed. She closes her eyes and sighs.

"That was wonderful," she says the words she has said many times, but this time they are true.

"But I am not done." At the humor in his voice, she opens her eyes again. He is smiling down on her, his teeth, glistening sharp, and dripping blood. She takes in a quick breath.

"I don't know your name..." it had never mattered before, "tell me your name...."

"You know my name. I am here to reawaken you."

And although she did not know his name before, she does now and feels an incomprehensible longing possess her. "Wulfstan," she whispers in wonder.

Quickly he reaches to his own chest, opens the skin with his nails and blood spurts onto Lizzie's face. She is shocked at his behavior, but he grasps her by the hair and forces her mouth into the wound. She gags at the taste of fresh blood, attempting to pull away from him, but he is too strong and she must eventually swallow his flow.

As the blood hits her stomach, she hears a laugh begin deep within her, it works its way up her throat and out of her mouth. Then suddenly, Lizzie Clayton is dead, murdered and I open my eyes to his smiling face.

There are still just the two of us, but we have been searching for the others. Surely they could be resurrected as we were. It makes no difference, Wulfstan says, we have plenty of time, all eternity. The world is ours and the food is plentiful.

OBSESSION

I

He's gone now. She can finally admit that to herself. More than a month and his traces have been washed away, even the wild scent of him that lingered in her nostrils, erased by the treacherous air she breathes. Yet still she waits; bound effectively by the silken cords he wove around her; gagged and speechless, blindfolded and sightless, possessed no longer by him, possessed only by the hunger he awoke. And the hunger he awoke and left unsatisfied now threatens to consume her from within. She longs for that consumption, she waits for that consumption.

Here is how she waits: naked in her betrayed bed, long hair spread upon a white pillowcase, his pillowcase, now unclaimed. Around the brass headboard she wraps a thin, red silk scarf, within which she entangles her wrists, as he would, were he there. Her eyes are covered, her breath muffled by the gag she wears. Toys, he once said, but they are now more than that. They have become her life.

There is no relief for her in this position, only the sweet torturing of remembered intimacies. And the listening for the key in the door, the step on the floor, the cool hand upon her breasts, her stomach. A breeze blows through the open window and chills her, teasing her nipples to erectness, raising fine hairs on her upper thighs. She would pull up the covers, but it is all part of the game she plays. She plays this game by the rules, his rules, lying exposed and ready for him, should he return. And no, it is not a game, it never was. He had a deadly seriousness that thrilled her, as if their sexual union meant more than life itself. And now, she realizes, that it did, if only to her.

A tear trickles from beneath her blindfold. She cannot wipe it away, it traces its way down her cheek. So like the sweat dropping from his brow as he worked over her body, his penis thrusting deep within her, relentless and demanding, searching out the hidden spots that others had missed. And what he demanded, she gave, would have continued to give until death took her. She would lick the sweat from his body, quenching her thirst, reveling in the taste of him, so different from the others, so exciting, so addictive. More tears now, like the flowing of the hot shower water, trickling over her back and her ass, as she knelt in front of him, worshipping him, wrapping her mouth around his cock and never wanting to have it gone; her arms around him, pushing on his ass to take all of him inside her, wanting him to gag her with that cock, wanting him to choke her with his seed. But his insistent hands dragged her to her feet and spun her around, so that he could take her from behind, his cock filling her entirely, impaling her completely. He'd put one hand on her hip, pulling, pushing, manipulating her body for his pleasure. The other tightly covered her mouth to muffle her screams and moans of delight.

As her tortured moans are muffled now, beneath the gag she wears for him, although he is not there. Slowly she unwinds her hands from the silken tangles, slowly and delicately as if this one transgression from the rules will go unnoticed. One hand travels to her left breast, twisting the nipple between her fingers, attempting to duplicate the effect of his mouth there. The nipple hardens and aches. Her other hand goes unerringly to her clitoris, erect now, aching also with a longing that echoes in her soul. She strokes herself, remembering the feel of his hand there, the expert touch that knew her body better than she did, the wetness of his tongue, the way his smoky eyes stared up at her, his head between her outstretched legs. Her cunt is wet and hot and empty; one finger inserted, even two cannot fill the void left by his cock. Her finger dips inside, collecting the wetness and works its way back to her clitoris, rubbing and stroking herself to orgasm after orgasm.

She makes little noise as she comes, the gag absorbing her breath and gasps. Her lips are dry, she would like remove the gag to moisten them. But that is not allowed. Only his tongue can lick the lips surrounding that thin strip of cloth, only his command can call for its removal. And he is gone.

She sighs and entwines her wrists once more within the scarf tied to the headboard. Listening and waiting, she spreads her legs wide so that she is exposed and ready for him again. Sightless and speechless, she falls asleep and dreams of his return.

II

The dreams of his return have all but disappeared. And her waking hopes seem dead and buried along with the sound of his name on her lips. The red silk scarf once cherished, like a widow's wedding veil, brought out at lonely times to stroke and savor the bittersweet reminder, is now ashes, burned in anger and thrown into the betraying wind that still would bring memories of him.

She thinks herself blessed, free of his presence, free of the pain of his love, his lies, his broken promises. But the passions that he awoke in her do not die that easily, they rage beneath the surface and burn visibly on her face, her body. She knows there can be no going back to her former life now; with or without him, she has been transformed, changed forever by the shiver of silk against her skin, the touch of his hands, and his mind.

She dresses with care: black skirt, full but sheer, revealing the shape of her legs, black sweater that clings so tightly to the curve of her breasts that she needs no bra, black hose and black heels. As she brushes her hair, she notices that her nipples are erect with excitement. Maybe tonight, she thinks, I will find a man to make me forget—forget myself, and erase his touch.

The motel bar is dark and smoky. A band is playing and after two drinks she dances, losing herself in a swirl of skirt and rhythm. Absorbed in the movement of her body and the warmth of the other bodies near her, she abandons all thought, becoming simply the sensuous sway of hips, the snakelike motions of arms and hands. She laughs, and spins, and laughs again. Then she feels a hand placed on her waist and she is turned around. The man is very tall and lean, with an arrogance about him that seems completely natural.

They dance and she grips his arms as if she were going to fall. She is faint, lightheaded from the muscular brush of his thighs on hers, from the pressure of his hardening penis held low against her stomach. He looks down at her, pulling her into his gaze, pulling her body closer still, until there is no space between his clothed flesh and hers.

She sighs, tenses briefly, then relaxes completely into his embrace. He laughs and his hands reach down to cup her ass, drawing her up against him. His mouth comes down on hers. It is a hard kiss, demanding and forceful, and she surrenders her mouth to his tongue, his teeth, knowing that it will only take one word from him to surrender herself completely.

She doesn't remember whether he spoke that one word, doesn't even remember how she came to be outside his room. There are only vague recollections of more dances, more drinks and a walk down the anonymous motel hallway. But she is here, nevertheless. He opens the door and holds it for her while she enters. He turns out the "Do not disturb" sign and closes the door.

She can feel the click of the lock deep down inside her and she shivers. Why is she here, with this man? Then he takes her in his arms, kisses her and she remembers. "Make me forget," she whispers to him and he laughs again, carrying her to the bed. He slides the shoes from her feet, tosses them to the floor and licks her nylon-clad soles and toes. She wiggles slightly then moans encouragement. He unzips her skirt, eases it down over her hips and drapes it over a chair. Then his fingers find the waistband of her hose, drawing them down over her legs. His hands are hot against her skin and her passions rise, her cunt grows wet and slippery. He takes his time and when her hose are removed, he puts a hand on each of her ankles and spreads her legs wide. His tongue begins slowly traveling up her inner leg, her thigh. She holds her breath, then exhales it in a gasp when his mouth touches her clitoris. He sucks her into him, licking her, while his hands reach up under her tight sweater and grasp her breasts. Her nipples are erect and he pinches them, gently at first, and then with more force.

She reaches down and pulls her sweater up over her head, throwing it across the room. He looks up at her, taking his mouth from her and smiles. Then his hands move away from her breasts and down once more to her cunt. He inserts one finger into her vagina, probing, thrusting, causing her to writhe and moan. Another finger joins it and his mouth comes down on her clitoris once more. With every touch of his tongue she shudders and spirals further down into the passion, until she comes, violently and loudly, thrashing about on the surface of the bed, one hand grasping the back of his head and the other pulling at the bed covers.

He pulls his head away and she groans, not wanting him to leave. His mouth bumps its way up her body, stopping at her nipples, pulling them deeply into his mouth, biting them, kneading both her breasts with his strong hands. She fears she will have bruises the next day, but is past caring. He lies on top of her, fully clothed, and grinds his erect penis into her groin. She arches her back and meets his thrusts. Then he rises from her and begins to unbutton his shirt.

"Let me," she whispers breathlessly. She kneels on the floor in front of him, removing his shirt first, then stretches her arms up, rubbing her palms over his chest. His skin and hair is silky beneath her fingers. She undoes his belt, his fly and pulls his pants down impatiently. He steps out of them, then gasps as she mouths his cock through his briefs. She feels it jump under her lips and she smiles as she removes his underwear. His cock is large, fully erect and this skin is silky, too. She rubs her cheek on it briefly, then runs her tongue around the tip and shaft. His taste is intriguing, male and sexy. She takes him entirely into her mouth, gagging slightly as she pulls him in. He thrusts into her, again and again. His action makes her wild and she grabs at his ass with one hand. The other finds its way between her legs and she rubs herself to climax again.

Finally, he takes hold of her hair and pulls her away from him. She moans her disappointment as he brings her up from her knees and holds her close to him again. Gently he urges her back to the bed, and sits her on the very edge, stroking her breasts, her hair, her cheek. He takes his cock into his hand, and guides just the tip into her, teasing her, teasing him, barely penetrating her vagina. She tries to thrust herself onto him, but he shakes his head.

"Slowly," he advises, "we have all night." Then he moves away, picking up her discarded pantyhose. "Lie back and hold your arms out, hands together," he says, his voice sounding deeper now, huskier and she obeys instantly, trembling only slightly. He wraps the hose around her wrists, then ties the ends to the headboard, leaving a small bit of slack. He stands back and looks down at her. "Very nice," he says, "all snug and secure."

She gives him a timid smile, and his hands travel over her body, not missing one inch of her exposed skin. "Yes," he says again, spreading her legs and climbing on top of her, "very nice."

He plunges deeply within her and she screams from the delight of the sensation. His skillful cock works inside her, thrusting forcefully, filling her, teasing her, coaxing her into one climax after another. Both their bodies are drenched in sweat when he finally withdraws, but he is still hard.

Grasping her hips in his hands, he quickly rolls her to her stomach. The slack in the hose that secures her to the headboard is now taken up and her arms are tightly bound. He helps her to get up to her knees, her movements are awkward since she has no use of hands or arms. He runs his hands over her back and ass, inserts a finger into her cunt and twirls it around, collecting her juices. Then he inserts the same finger into her anus, gently, but insistently, until she is opened to him. With his finger still inside her ass, he drives his cock back into her vagina, working it deeply in until it is drenched. She bucks herself back into him, the feel of both finger and cock is driving her crazy. Then he pulls out of her cunt. She feels the cool unctuousness of lube on her skin, hears the sound of it being smoothed over her skin, and worked into her ass. She sighs and shivers and he inserts the head of his sopping cock into her anus. Slowly, so as not to hurt her, he works his entire length into her and begins to thrust in and out. One hand reaches around and twists at each of her nipples, the other plays at her clitoris. She climaxes again and again, and he starts to pound her frantically, fucking her ass as hard as he fucked her cunt. His hands grasp at her hips, pulling her back and forth, onto him and off again, until finally with one loud groan and gasp, he comes. The feel of his semen shooting deep into her bowels causes her to come again, her knees give out beneath her and he collapses onto her back.

He nuzzles her neck briefly before pulling out, unties her hands and lies down next to her. She snuggles in close to him, one arm draped over his chest and sighs.

"Well," he says, laughter in his voice, "don't you have anything to say."

"Make me forget, again."

III

She sits at an open window; the storm that rages outside is nothing compared to the one within her heart. The lightning, the wind, the rain blowing onto her face through the screen: all of these remind her of him. There is no forgetting, she fears, and no getting over this obsession. Her attempts to erase the memory and purge him from her body and soul have failed, leaving only guilt and tears and a longing strong enough to rip her apart.

The bitterness and anger she once felt toward him is now directed inward. She knows where the true blame lies. The grasping meanness, the angry words that drove him away were hers alone. The attempt to hold him past the time he wished to be held was not for her to make. They had struck a bargain, an agreement to no permanent commitment and she'd been the one to renege.

"But," she whispers into the wind, "Didn't you know that your words of love canceled that bargain? And didn't you know that I was fighting for my life?"

There is no answer, how can there be? But the wildness he awoke within her is called to by the storm. She unfastens her robe, drops her nightgown off her shoulders and unlocks the door, walking naked into the night.

Her nipples are whipped into instant erectness by the wind and the heat of her body is soothed by the down pouring of cold rain. She dances now as she danced before, spinning and twirling to an internal rhythm, her pale skin illuminated by flashes of lightning, her hair, coiling wet and tangled around her face and down her back. But now there is no other man here to help her forget; she is alone, as she knows she will always be.

"Forget," whispers the wind. "He is gone," shouts the rain. Still she dances on and on, water streaming down her face, caressing her nakedness. "I will not forget," her voice trembles, small yet determined over the thunder, "he is gone, but I will not forget."

He had been a magical presence in her life, before he left. Even separated by time and distance, she could feel him with her, hear his thoughts. He had imprinted himself on her completely, his possession of her had been so absolute that it only took the thought of him to bring back the sensation of him, thrusting deep within her cunt or her mouth, the touch of his hands probing and stroking, the taste of his skin and his sweat. She needed only to close her eyes to see his face, see his muscular and hard body working over her.

Now she can see nothing through the sheeting rain. Instead, she strains to hear a voice, traveling through the storm. "I'd like to make love to you, one more time." She knows that voice, knows that it can only come from deep inside her, knows that it means only madness and obsession, but does not care.

"Come here."

Obediently, silently, she lies down by a tree, the tree underneath which he had once loved her, so long ago, when he'd awakened and found her gone, when her absence in his bed had been like a void in his soul and in panic he'd gone to search for her. She had been sitting under the tree clad only in a thin white nightgown watching the clear sky when he found her. And they'd made love—it was love she insists in her memory—his hands had been so strong, so demanding, laying her down in the damp grass, lifting up her gown, his hands and mouth and body exploring her, as if in her small absence from his side, she had changed and he needed to discover her once again. She remembers how he had played at her breasts, deeply sucking her nipple into his mouth, how his smoky eyes had stared up at her, pulling her into him. He had worshipped her body that night, neglecting no part of her, giving her spasm after spasm of pleasure, before grasping her ankles in his hands and driving his cock deep inside her, pulsing, thrusting, filling her with his seed and his love.

Now nothing touches her but the rain. She closes her eyes tightly and stretches her arms over her head, memories providing the feel of the red silk scarf wrapped around her wrists. She spreads her legs wide and the rain falls harder, pummeling her body. She arches up to meet the weather's caress and allows it to love her, since he is gone. It touches her like a lover, the thunder speaks to her and the lightning illuminates her body. The rain laps at her clitoris, licks at her breasts, covering her completely, passionately. She opens her mouth and allows the rain to enter there, the gush of water down her throat so like his semen, gagging her in its insistent rush.

Her hands travel from their imaginary bonds and run themselves over her wet skin, pausing at her erect nipples, then their nails lightly trace their way down to her cunt. Still thrusting upward to meet the kiss of the sky, she inserts one finger then two into her throbbing vagina; she is hot and wet and her muscles contract around her fingers tightly as she comes, coaxed into orgasm by the rain.

She gasps and thrashes, her small noises covered by the tossing of branches in the wind. After a while she lies quiet, as does the storm, calmer now, gentler, washing away for a time her ache and pain. The sky begins to lighten and dawn is close. She rises, wrings out her sopping hair and enters the house, pausing at the open door long enough to whisper, "Goodbye."

THE PRESENCE

I remember that first day as the turning point, as one of the most beautiful days of my life. The sun shone warmly, it could almost have been summer except for the cold wind that blew my long blonde hair into a cloud of tangles. But it was spring and the earth seemed to be bursting with vitality. I felt that if I stood in one place too long, its infectious growth would flow up my limbs and I would take root like—oh, what the hell was her name ... Apollo and ... and ... oh, yeah—"Daphne."

"Miss Hawthorne?"

I jumped slightly and glanced at Jonathan Weber, my future landlord, scarcely realizing I had spoken. Not wanting him to think I was too eccentric—he's no Apollo, but he might do in a pinch—I pushed the hair from my eyes and gave him a warm smile. "Nothing, I was just sort of thinking out loud. I'm sorry, you were saying?"

He was substantially taller than I, probably at least a foot, and his dark hair, only slightly grey, was tousled from the wind. His brown eyes danced as he became aware of my scrutiny and he returned my smile encouragingly. "I said that the utility bills are generally higher in the winter. With all those windows..." he shrugged and pointed to the third floor apartment of the Victorian-style home. "But of course, that's why you want it. The light is wonderful for painting. I believe it was used by the original owner as a studio, also."

I looked to where the sunlight glinted from the row of windows and felt a shiver of anticipation. "It's perfect," I whispered to myself and my fingers tingled, aching for the brush, the smooth, sensuous sweep of oil across canvas. "Let's go up," I tugged on his sleeve like an impatient child, "I want to see the inside."

He began to climb an outer set of stairs and I followed eagerly. The entrance to the enclosed set of stairs was unlocked and he opened the door and paused on the landing. "You can lock this if you want; the couple living in the second floor apartment," and he gestured to a closed door opposite the entrance, "have a complete set of keys. I expect it probably seems strange, with you coming from a big city like New York, but many people around here still leave their doors open. We've very little crime here, even though the town has expanded a bit." He shrugged and smiled at me, then climbed the last flight of stairs, opening the door to my new apartment and holding it back to allow me to enter first.

Five more steps up and I was there. The first thing I noticed was the smell of fresh paint and new carpeting. Underneath those odors I thought I detected a heady floral scent, exotic and seductive. And despite the wash of sunlight coming through the windows, the room was cold, icy cold. I walked into the living area, folding my arms across my chest so that the tightening of my nipples would not be so obvious.

The apartment was ideal, not as compact as the place I had moved from, and not large enough to be a burden. The kitchen, though small, had been completely modernized, as had the bath. The bedroom was merely a curtained alcove adjacent to the main area. But the studio was well-lit, airy and exactly as he had described it to me. Once again I felt the urge to begin painting at once, even though the bulk of my supplies would not arrive until tomorrow.

Jonathan cleared his throat nervously and I turned, surprised to see that he was still standing at the top of the stairs, not completely in the apartment. "This is a wonderful place," I said, "I just can't believe my luck in finding it vacant. Thank you."

"Well," he smiled hesitantly, "it's like I tried to explain to you in our correspondence, not too many people have felt comfortable here. I really hope it's different for you."

"You've never been to New York, have you?"

He shook his head, "No, but what has that got to do with anything?"

My laughter seemed to puzzle him, so I continued. "Well, compared to the places I've been, the people I've roomed with and the sights I've seen, your ghost should be a welcome change." I tried unsuccessfully to hide my skepticism. I did not believe in ghosts. "So tell me, does he appear at midnight, moaning and clanking his chains? Or does he just throw sharp objects at the people who intrude in his space?"

He shook his head with vehemence, almost indignantly. "No, of course not. It's really nothing like that; if it were I would close the place off, or," and his face held the trace of a smile, "maybe I'd sell tickets. I don't know if I would even go so far as to call it a ghost; at the most it's a presence, or maybe just the residue of strong emotions. No one, to my knowledge, has ever seen anything. People stay for a few months, then find a reason to leave. It's never anything specific."

"Whatever it is, I'm not worried about it. So don't you worry either. I'll be fine, honestly. And I'd feel quite at home if only it were just a bit warmer."

"Oh, God, I'm sorry. I can fix that up pretty quickly." He seemed to relax finally and walked across the room to the radiator. "Like I said, Miss Hawthorne, I hope you'll stay," he glanced over at me shyly while he adjusted the heat, "it's an honor to have a beautiful and talented artist staying here."

"Call me Mara," I said, suddenly embarrassed at his compliment, and was startled to hear the name whispered back to me.

He gave the radiator a kick with his foot, "You'll get used to this thing after a while. It makes a lot of noise sometimes." As if in response to his statement, the radiator hissed again, a close enough approximation of my name that I realized what had happened.

I laughed as he moved to the steps, "You know, Jonathan, I don't think you have a ghost at all; just a noisy heating system."

"Maybe," he gestured to the telephone, "but if you have any trouble, please give me a call. My number's on a card next to the phone. And I do live on the first floor, so if you have an emergency, you can just run down and get me." He walked over to me and extended his hand. I shook it; he had a nice grip, firm but gentle and I felt that he held my hand just a little bit longer than necessary.

"Thank you, Jonathan. I'm sure everything will be fine."

"Do you want some help with your stuff?" Although he had been reluctant about coming into the apartment now it seemed that he didn't want to leave. I wondered if he enjoyed my company that much, or if he was just concerned about the ghost making an appearance and frightening off a steady rental income.

"No, thanks anyway. All I have is a small suitcase and my iPod. Everything else should arrive tomorrow. And since I won't be sleeping here tonight, I think I'll just look around a bit more and head over to the motel."

"Did I warn you about the connectivity problems here?"

I smiled at him. "Yes, several times during our correspondence. And as I said, I'm good with that. For a while, anyway. I don't own a television set, I cancelled my cell phone contract before leaving the city, and closed down all of my email and social accounts."

Jonathan winced. "That seems a bit drastic."

I nodded. "But a fresh start isn't fresh if you drag around all of the old shit with you, is it?" I didn't feel obligated to give him an explanation. He didn't need to know the hell of past relationships I was escaping. But I smiled again. "Anyway, I'm sure there are places I can use the internet if I need to."

"Sure, lots of them." He hesitated a second and the temperature seemed to drop again. Jonathan shook his head and headed to the door. "Okay then, you take care."

I followed him and he turned around and handed me two sets of keys. "Here you go," he said, "I guess I'll see you around." He walked out, closed the door behind him and I was alone.

Pushing the keys into the back pocket of my jeans, I slowly walked into the studio. Sheer lace curtains that diffused the sunlight and traced delicate shadowy webs on the walls and tiled floor covered the wide expanse of windows, flanking the long wall of the room. Beneath the windows was a long upholstered bench; I sat down and pulled the curtains to one side. I was relieved to see that there were no houses across the street, just an overgrown swatch of trees and brush. "Good," I said aloud, "then there's no one to spy on me when I want to paint in the nude." Shivering, I realized that there would be no nudity here until the heat improved. I rubbed my hands up and down the raised flesh on my arms and, rising from the window seat, went into the other room to check out the closets.

They were more than adequate; my wardrobe was almost completely limited to jeans, t-shirts and sweaters, including only two dresses for gallery appearances and the like. My life style was Bohemian, but it suited me fine.

I stopped in the bathroom and tried out the plumbing. When I finished, I could again smell the floral scent I had first noted. When I explored the kitchen, the mystery solved itself. Lying on the window ledge, at the end of the dormer, was a single rose, open and fragrant. "How nice," I said as I picked it up and inhaled. "I'll have to remember to thank Jonathan."

"Ahhraa..." the radiator hissed again as I walked past it on my way to the door.

"Don't worry," I whispered, patting the ironwork with a grin for my foolishness, "you just get this place warm and I'll be back tomorrow."

The movers were late. I had arrived as agreed by eight, and after unpacking what clothes and few toiletries I carried with me, waited by the windows in the studio. I was slightly hungover from an evening spent discussing modern art with the bartender at my motel. For someone living in this backwater town, he had proven to be fairly well versed with some of my more popular compatriots; this surprised me until I found out that he was a graduate student from a university in a nearby town. And when he discovered that I did representational art, not "those godawful paint splatters," he had kept my glass filled until the bar closed.

He'd wanted to come back to my room, but I slept alone, having learned the hard way not to trust my judgment about men after a few drinks. That was the way I had become involved with so many men, especially my ex-husband; he was the main reason I'd moved from the city, hoping for an escape from his continual leeching of my money, my self-respect, and my emotional reserves.

I stretched a bit, having become cramped sitting and watching out the windows, sorry that my thoughts had brought me back to past relationships. "Okay, you bastards," I said with a bitter laugh, shifting my position to lay down flat on the window seat, "just try and find me here." I crossed my arms behind my head and studied the shadows of the lace curtains on the ceiling. The sun streaming through the windows warmed my face, soothed my throbbing head, and lulled me to sleep.

Somehow my thoughts of gods the day before became twisted up with my musings about the men I had known. I was Daphne and they took turns as Apollo, chasing me, leading me back to this apartment, strangely furnished and heavily scented with the overpowering aroma of a thousand roses. When he caught me, it seemed different somehow, because he was different and everything was finally okay. He promised me, oh, he promised me so much, all I had ever wanted, an eternity of love and fidelity.

"Forever, Mara," he whispered, his breath causing the hair on the back of my neck to rise, causing delicate shivers to undulate through my willing body. "This will be forever."

"Yes," I agreed and moaned as his hands caressed my breasts through my thin shirt, teasing the nipples to an aching erectness. "You're cold," I murmured, "you are so cold."

"But you will warm me, my lovely one." His hands fumbled with the zipper of my jeans and, in spite of their icy touch, I felt the answering gush of warmth from within me. "I need you," he urged as he slid my panties down my thighs, "I love you. Give yourself to me, Mara."

"Yes," I gasped, "yes." The weight of his body on mine was exciting, yet comforting, as if it were something I had been awaiting all my life. But when I reached my arms up to pull him down to me, they found nothing. "Where are you?" I asked desperately, struggling to open my sleep-sealed eyes, "I can't touch you."

"No," he said, a heavy sadness in his voice as tangible as the fragrance and the cold, "you cannot touch me. Yet."

A loud knocking on the door woke me, and I sat up, disoriented and trembling. My jeans lay on the floor in a crumpled heap and my panties were tangled around my ankles. My shirt was bunched up around my neck and as I pulled it down I noticed the small reddened patches on my breasts. "Jesus," I swore as I hurriedly dressed to let the movers in, "that was one hell of a dream."

I waited impatiently as the movers unloaded my meager assortment of furniture. The first piece of furniture to come off the truck was my bed, an antique brass piece that had been in my family for generations. Although over the years it had undergone many renovations—the entire undercarriage had been rewired, and new springs and supports were installed—it still creaked dreadfully with even normal sleeping movements. The noise it made during more strenuous use was incredible, but I didn't really mind. Especially not here, I reminded myself, trying to shake loose of the strange, erotic dream I'd had. I hadn't come to this two-bit town to pursue relationships or sex. I'd come to paint.

Sitting on the edge of the bare mattress, one leg crossed under me and the other swinging free, I casually directed the placement of the rest of the furniture. The two chairs, the end table and an old lamp went into the living room, the dresser, along with another lamp, older still, to the right of my bed and the dinette table and two folding chairs, into the kitchen. Following the furniture were five cartons labeled 'miscellaneous household items' containing mostly kitchen goods and linens and two large suitcases containing my clothes. I ran my fingers idly through my tangled hair as I watched, not really caring where any of these items went. But when one of the movers came up the stairs with the first large crate marked 'canvases,' I jumped off the bed and, to the obvious disgust of the workers, became actively involved in the process of unloading.

Finally, when all my supplies had been unpacked and accounted for on the bill of lading, I signed for the shipment and the movers left. I was anxious to get started; my thoughts the other day of gods in pursuit, not to mention that incredible dream, had inspired me to start a series of mythological-based paintings, all portraying the romance of the supernatural.

"Although, let's be realistic, Mara," I told myself as I stripped off my jeans and donned an oversized painting shirt, "romance is just a euphemistic term for what you really have in mind. What we're talking about here is lust - all those hot, sweaty bodies intertwined." Pulling a large canvas out of the stack, I laughed a little, remembering some of the reviews my last show had received from the more conservative papers. "Too much exposed flesh," one had said. And "a flagrant and graphic depiction of sexual acts, bordering on pornography," said another.

"And you know what?" I crossed the room and turned up the radiator, "I sold every stinking one of them. People were literally panting for more."

The radiator hissed out a little sigh, "Ahhraa," and I patted it.

"That's right, baby, just give me a little more heat and I'll take care of the sex."

Walking back into the studio, I paced a bit, considering the empty canvas. I decided that the first painting would be of Daphne and

Apollo, since they hadn't actually consummated their relationship. That way each progressive canvas could accelerate the process ending in the ultimate seduction of ... oh, hell, I don't know who, I thought, I'm going to need to do research on this sucker.

It didn't really matter, I had enough information to paint the first scene and inspiration would follow. It always did. But I made a mental note to check with Jonathan Weber about the nearest library so that I could either get a book or check online. In the meantime, I could simply concentrate on Daphne.

How would she feel, I wondered, setting out my tubes of oil and preparing a few brushes, being pursued by a god? Would she be flattered by his attention, but secure enough in herself to believe she could escape him? Wouldn't she even be just a little bit curious wondering about what it would be like, how his mouth would feel on hers, his hands on her breasts, the size of his....

"Get real, Mara," I said out loud, "she was a virgin, and had vowed to remain one. What the hell did she care about the size of the man's penis?" Snorting to myself, I began to block out the picture, mixing a delicate pink flesh color for Daphne, a darker color for Apollo's skin and sketching in suggestions of their bodies and the flowers and forest in the background.

As always I became immersed in my work and long hours passed before I stopped, suddenly conscious of the darkening windows and a gnawing hunger. The apartment seemed cold now, although my shirt was drenched with sweat. I peeled it off and went into the bathroom for a shower.

Turning the water up as hot as it would go, I let it run for a few minutes to build up the warmth in the room. I brushed my teeth while I waited, watching through the mirror as the puffs of steam billowed, eventually blocking the vision of myself. A childhood fear returned to me as I bent over the sink and rinsed my mouth, someone could be standing right behind me and I would never know. Even as I thought it, I shivered. "Jesus, Mara, you're letting this haunted house business get to you on your first night here. You've got more sense than that."

Nevertheless, I couldn't control a furtive glance over my shoulder before getting into the shower. But when the hot water hit my tired body it soothed and comforted and I relaxed as I soaped myself. When I washed my breasts, I noticed small bruises around the nipples, but dismissed them. My skin was extremely fair and delicate; I was always turning up bruised in the oddest places, never remembering what I had done to cause it.

I dried myself, took a blow dryer to my hair, and put on a clean pair of jeans and a bulky sweater. Then I picked up my keys and my purse and bounded down the many flights of stairs to the street outside. Jonathan's light was on, so I walked up the few steps of his front porch and rang his bell.

"Hi," I said, when he answered the door. "I don't mean to be a pest, but I was wondering if you could tell me where the library is in this town. And if you could point me to a good restaurant nearby, I'd be eternally grateful."

"No problem," he pulled off the pair of reading glasses he'd been wearing, stuffed them impatiently into his shirt pocket, and checked his watch. "Library's closed right now. And you don't really want to use the one in town anyway. The college's is better." He rubbed his eyes slightly, and when he looked at me again, his eyes seemed tired and red.

"I'm sorry," I said quickly, embarrassed that I had interrupted him, "did I come at a bad time?"

"No, no, not at all. I was just grading some term papers."

"Oh, you're a teacher? I didn't know that."

"I'm a professor at the college, actually. What did you think I did for a living?"

I gave him a wry smile, "I didn't really think of you having a profession. I just guessed that your leasing apartments was enough."

Jonathan laughed. "Oh, come on. Your rent isn't that high, is it? How on earth do you think I could make a living out of it?"

"Maybe I visualized you as the slum-landlord of this place."

"Thanks a lot," he said dryly.

"You're welcome." I paused a minute, then continued, "What do you teach?"

"Antiquities," he said apologetically, then shrugged, "I know, it's boring as all get out."

"No," I thought of my current fascination with mythology, and gave him a warm smile, "I don't think it's boring at all, Jonathan. But I don't want to hold you up any longer. And I'm starving."

"Let me get my coat. I'll be right with you."

"Oh, no, I didn't mean to...." I blushed slightly at the thought that he might think I was fishing for a dinner invitation.

He came back with his coat and looked at me with shy amusement. I blushed more deeply, knowing that he noticed my embarrassment. "Oh, I'm sure you didn't," he said, closing and locking his door, "but I did."

We walked three blocks into the main thoroughfare of the town and stopped at the traffic light.

"Well, what would you like to eat?" Jonathan pointed to his right, "Over here we have pizza, burgers, and health food. And," he spun around and pointed the other way, "over here is the diner, and a steak and spaghetti joint."

I looked at him with his arms out flung and began to laugh.

"What's so funny?"

"You look like the scarecrow from the Wizard of Oz."

"I do?" He looked down at himself then gave a boyish grin and dropped his arms. "Yeah, I guess I do. And you haven't even seen me fall down yet."

We stood silently for a minute waiting for the light to change. "The scarecrow, huh? Is that good?"

"Depends," I said, still chuckling to myself.

"On what?"

"On whether the diner serves an authentic cherry cola or not."

"Well, you're in luck, young lady. The diner it is."

The light changed and he tentatively put a hand on my waist as if to guide me. When I did not avoid the contact but leaned into him as we crossed, his grip grew stronger.

The diner was crowded but we got the last available booth. The server greeted him by name and he ordered our drinks first so that I could have time to look at the menu. When she brought the sodas, I tore open the straw, took one long sip and sighed in contentment.

"Authentic enough for you?"

"It's wonderful." I took another sip and went back to the menu. A shadow fell over us and I looked up to see a young girl standing hesitantly, waiting for someone to notice her.

"Dr. Weber?" Her voice cracked a bit over his name. Her hands were stuffed into her pockets and she looked as if she had been crying.

"Susan." Jonathan's voice acquired a sharpness and directness I would not have thought possible for him. I gave him a curious glance as he glared at the poor girl.

"I, I need to talk to you," she looked down at me, her eyes studying my face carefully before darting back to his, "about my grade, you know."

"Yes, I know." His tone softened a bit, but still sounded imperative, authoritative. "But my office hours are tomorrow." He pulled a small calendar out of his shirt pocket. "I'm free from one to three. You should come by then."

She was obviously too young to hear the finality in his voice. "But, it's important, and I thought that...."

"Tomorrow, Susan. From one to three."

She stood almost defiantly in front of us for a few final seconds, then her shoulders drooped and she walked to a booth further in the back of the diner. I watched her as she slid into her seat, her back to us. The other girl she was sitting with shook her head and from the expression on her face I got the impression she was scolding Susan. I wished I could read lips.

"Mara?" Jonathan's voice was apologetic now. "I'm sorry we were interrupted. Students just can't seem to get the idea that I'm not available twenty-four hours a day."

"She's very pretty." I didn't mean anything by the comment but that. Jonathan shifted in his seat uneasily.

"Yes, I suppose she is. But," he spoke faster than normal, "her grades are atrocious and her grasp of the material non-existent. I've been helping her as much as I could, giving her special tutoring, but she doesn't seem to get it." Then he shrugged and smiled. "We don't really need to discuss this, tonight, do we? I get enough of it during working hours."

"No," I said agreeably, "let's talk about something other than your job."

Even if he hadn't seemed relieved at my dismissal of the subject, I was glad to move on to other matters. I didn't know him well enough to want to get involved with his students or his academic career. What he did really made very little difference to me.

The server came by and took our dinner orders. After she left, Jonathan looked over at me. "How'd everything go today?"

"Fine, thanks. The movers were so late that I fell asleep waiting for them, but other than that...." My voice trailed away as I remembered the dream I'd had. The fragrance of the roses, the touch of those cold hands on me, the instant response of my body, the way I must have undressed myself in my sleep.... Jesus, Mara, I thought, blushing furiously at the thought of how aroused I had been, how aroused even just the memory could make me, calm down. Don't work yourself into a sexual frenzy about some stupid dream.

"Mara? Come back, you're miles away."

I opened my eyes to Jonathan's face. His confusion was apparent, as was his concern.

"I'm sorry," I said, feeling confused myself. My stomach was tight, my heart racing and I began to tremble.

"Are you cold?" He stood up and took his jacket off. "Here," he said, moving quickly to my side of the booth, "put this on." In a chivalrous manner, he draped it over my shoulders and I pulled it tight around me.

"Thanks," I smiled and slid over on the seat as he sat down next to me. "I guess I did get a sort of chill. You really should do something about the heat up there."

"I'll check it tonight for you, if you want." His voice was warm and caressing and I gave him a sidelong glance, thinking that he was probably not much interested in the radiator, thinking, also, that an evening with him would probably be full of sexual revelations. But I'd resolved not to get involved with another man. And for some reason, the thoughts of his entering that apartment with me were frightening.

"Not tonight, Jonathan." My voice quavered just a bit and I cleared my throat. "But thanks anyway, maybe I could have a rain check."

"Sure thing. Anytime." His voice was calm and confident, as if he was unaware that I'd just turned him down. I glanced at him again. Maybe he was unaware, maybe it was just a friendly offer to help.

"So," I said, abruptly changing the subject, "what did you do today?"

"Now, we already agreed not to discuss my job. But how about you? Why don't you tell me about your paintings?"

I gave a small laugh. "No, that's no good, either. I don't really like to talk about what I do. Especially when I'm working on a project."

"Oh," his eyes lit with curiosity, "have you started painting already? What are you..." he caught himself mid-sentence and laughed. "Sorry. So what are we going to talk about?"

"Well," I said hesitantly, "I suppose we could talk about your ghost." Now what on earth possessed me to say that, I thought, there is no ghost.

"I'm not sure I've too much to say about him. Like I told you yesterday, no one has actually ever seen anything. Or if they have, they never told me about it."

"But you must have some idea who it is; I mean, you did say 'him' as if you knew the ghost was a man. And the house can't have had all that many owners, you should be able to narrow it down a bit."

"I thought you didn't believe in ghosts," he said.

"I don't. I was just trying to find something to talk about. And it's sort of fun to consider the possibility, don't you think? I've never lived in a haunted house before. It might be interesting."

"You're a weird one, Mara Hawthorne. I guess it must be your artistic temperament."

The server brought our food and Jonathan went to sit back opposite me. We ate silently for a while. The food was standard diner fare, but I'd never been particular about what I ate as long as someone else cooked it.

"Is your meal okay?"

"Great, thank you." I took one last bite and pushed my plate away.

"So tell me about yourself. Your parents, your childhood, why you decided to become an artist, things like that."

I gave a small, cynical laugh. "I don't think you ever decide to become an artist, as you put it. You're either one or you aren't; there's no middle ground." I shifted on my seat and leaned back into the corner of the booth. "My parents died when I was only five and I was shuffled around from foster home to foster home for the next thirteen years. Oh," I said quickly, trying to forestall the expressions of sympathy that usually followed my history, "it's not really as bad as it sounds. I barely remember my mom and dad; I have a few pictures and I know their names, but the memories just aren't there. And it was an interesting way to grow up, I suppose."

"Why weren't you ever adopted? You must have been a beautiful little girl."

I laughed. "Actually, nothing could be further from the truth. I was too skinny, too pale, too quiet, too placid..." I thought of all the other criticisms I'd endured over the years, "...well, you get the idea. I never matched up with anyone in particular; then one family, the MacIntyres, finally got tired of me scratching intricate designs into their furniture and drawing on their walls and sent me for art lessons. Things were easier after that, because I'd finally found something that I was good at. It didn't stop them from sending me on when my time was up, but, thank God, all the families I stayed with afterward kept up the classes. I can still hear the social worker telling each subsequent one, 'The art makes her easier to manage.'"

He reached over and held my hand briefly. "And so an artist was born."

"Yeah," I said and pulled my hand away from him, embarrassed that I'd told him so much. "So how about you? What was your family like?"

"Pretty normal, I guess."

The server brought our check and Jonathan paid it.

"It's bad enough that I dragged you away from your papers," I protested, "the least you can let me do is pay."

"Some other time," Jonathan got up and I followed him out of the diner.

On our walk home the wind began to gust, whipping wildly through the trees that lined the sidewalks.

"It'll rain tonight." He sounded so confident that I laughed.

"Oh, I see. Being a professor and a slumlord isn't enough. Now you want to be a weather man."

"Actually, you don't have to live here very long to make that prediction. It either rains or snows ten months out of the year in this town. And," he put his arms around me as we reached his front steps, "it's not cold enough tonight to snow."

In spite of my previous resolution, I responded eagerly when his mouth came down on mine. Jonathan Weber's kiss contradicted his shy, distracted manner. He was experienced—no question about that—he was very experienced and his hands sought out the exact places on my back and torso to stroke and touch. He pulled me closer into him and I could feel his arousal pressed hard against me. His lips were persistent, demanding and I wanted nothing more than to melt into his arms. But, I reminded myself with regret, I don't want a relationship, not here and not now, and I pushed away from him reluctantly. My breath came in soft pants as I shook my head.

"Rain check?" he asked, not angrily, but in a matter-of-fact tone, as if what he wanted were something as simple to give away as a cup of coffee. He smoothed an unruly strand of hair away from my face and his smile was so boyish, so seemingly innocent that I almost changed my mind.

A powerful gust of wind interrupted us and we both jumped at the loud crash behind us.

"What the hell?" he said, spinning around and staring at the shutter that had come loose in the wind and had fallen only a few feet behind him. "Damn," he turned back to me, a shocked expression erasing the passion from his face, "that could have hit us dead on."

My heart was pounding but I managed a shaky laugh. "I'll have to tell my landlord about this."

"Yeah," Jonathan said, laughing as well, "you do that."

"Anyway," I began, anxious suddenly to get upstairs, out of the brutal wind, "I had a nice time. Thank you."

"My pleasure, Mara." He moved toward me, but I backed away to the steps leading to the third floor.

"See you later, Jonathan."

"Oh, Mara," he called after me, "feel free to use the library up at the college. I'll sign for you."

"Thank you." I almost had to scream to be heard over the wind, but I didn't want to get any closer to him.

"What did you need to look up?"

God, doesn't he ever stop trying? "I need to look up some mythology. I could do it online...." I hesitated, not sure I could resist contacting the bad influences I was trying to escape. "Or I could just look at a copy of Bullfinch's *Mythology*."

"What?" He came toward me and took my arm, guiding me to the steps. The side of the house provided some shelter from the wind, so I repeated my request as we walked up the stairs together.

"No problem," he replied, "I can easily find a copy of that downstairs. Come on back down...."

I interrupted him. "Thanks, tomorrow would be fine." I put my key into the door in a totally unsubtle hint, "I'd like to get some sleep now."

"Good night, Mara." Finally sensing my mood he made no further advances, but leaned toward me with a mischievous smile. "Oh, and Mara?"

"Yeah?"

"His name is probably Owen Culver."

"Whose name?" I couldn't follow his reasoning. Bullfinch's name was probably Owen Culver?

"The ghost. His name is Owen Culver." He turned away and hurried down the stairs. The rain began to pound on the roof as I entered my apartment, turning on the hall light and chuckling to myself at Jonathan's cleverness. He knew I would have to see him again to get the full story.

Still laughing, I shook my head as I locked the door. "Owen Culver, huh? But it won't work, Jonathan, I won't invite you in tonight to tell me about it." The rain continued to fall, heavier now and a flash of lightning lit the room brightly. When the flash was over, the room was in total darkness. "Great," I said, stumbling into the kitchen to find the candles I knew I had packed away somewhere, "just stinking great. My first night here and no lights."

The candles were, of course, in the very last box I chose to search. Finally, when I had them lit and set around the apartment, I'd enough light to find my way around, but not enough, I realized, to paint. I went back into the kitchen and pulled out a set of sheets and a blanket from the linens box and made the bed. Then I unpacked a few more of the cartons, stopping when I found a large plastic tumbler and the bottle of scotch. I went to the living room and curled up in my favorite armchair, drinking and watching the rain run down the studio windows.

It must have been quite a few hours later when I woke; the storm had calmed, my glass of scotch was on the floor and several of the candles had gone out, but at least the overhead light was back on. I stretched and got out of the chair, going to the lamp on my dresser and turning it on. Then I went back to the entryway and turned out the overhead switch. Blowing out the remaining candles, I stopped at the radiator and adjusted the knob again. A burst of warmed air hit me and I smiled, stripping off my clothes. I had been hoping that I would not have to wear anything to bed; I preferred to sleep the way I painted: in the nude. "Thank you," I whispered as I turned out the lamp, "and good night to you, Owen Culver, whoever the hell you are."

The scent of the candles I had extinguished followed me into my dreams and once again I was in a strange version of the apartment. The furniture was different, not the old pieces of junk I had brought, but beautifully restored antiques. Where the overhead light had been now hung a beautiful crystal chandelier, the flames of its candles dancing in the warm spring breeze, glass prisms sighing their tingling music through the room. Flowers, drooping with heavy blooms, flooded my senses with their warm, exotic scents. I sighed, it was all so beautiful, so much more fitting than before, and I felt as if I had finally, after all those long years, arrived home.

Wrapping the top sheet around my naked body, I sat up in bed, unmistakably my bed by the creaking and groaning of the springs. Everything else around me was different, except the canvas I had started that afternoon set up in the studio. I squinted at it across the room and saw that it, too, had changed; the figure of Apollo was more defined, more real, than I had painted. And Daphne looked more like me than I remembered.

How interesting, I thought, I must see it closer. But a warm languor overcame me and I was unable get out of bed. Instead, I settled back on the pillows and threw back the sheets. Looking down at my naked body, I compared it to the painting. Yes, she is very much like me, and I ran my hands along the contours of my breasts, my stomach, my upper thighs, as if through exploring my own body, I could gain a better understanding of hers. All the while, the eyes of Apollo seemed to fasten on me; eyes of flashing electric blue, watching my movements intently, hungrily.

I gasped. They were devouring eyes, inhuman eyes that I could never have painted, eyes that would have driven me away screaming if I were awake. It's only a dream. That thought relaxed me, because when I knew it was a dream, I was not afraid. The sensuality of his stare, the way his eyes lingered caressingly on my lips and breasts, and the promises those eyes held—days and nights of love and lust and unimaginable passion—intrigued me, aroused me, made me hot and desperate, oh God, so desperate for the touch of another pair of hands.

I should have invited Jonathan in, I thought, as my body writhed and my back arched in invitation to anyone that could ease the teasing torment. There could be no easing, since no one was there.

"I don't want to be alone," I half groaned the words. "I want someone, anyone, I don't care who."

As if my words had weight to touch the air around me, the chandelier rocked back and forth, several of the candles blew out and the prisms jangled discordantly. In the flickering light, the figure that had been watching me from the painting seemed to move, the outlines wavered as if a veil had passed over them, or had fallen away. I should be frightened, I thought, I should call for help, but my voice froze in my throat, and the hot, sensual languor still held control of my body. I licked my lips as I stared at the wispy outline of the man and my breath came in soft, short gasps. "You're only a dream," I breathed to him over the scented air, "but I don't care. I want you, come to me."

The touch on my foot was barely perceptible at first, except as an easing, a cooling for my blazing flesh. I sighed and closed my eyes, savoring the sensation. Cold fingers crawled up my ankle, slowly caressed the skin of my knees, and lingered there, teasing and tantalizing.

"Mara," the whispering of my name thrilled my entire body, "Mara."

The cool touch of his breath on my skin caused me to cry out in incoherent longing. The ghostly fingers seemed warmer as if the fire of my flesh had given them life, and they traveled further up my legs, kneading my thighs. And when they finally reached and thrust deeply into the center of my body's heat, I was completely lost, beyond knowing this for a dream, beyond caring who or what he was.

"Ah," I breathed, "so good, so good, never wake up...."

I was answered only by a deeper probing and an almost imperceptible laugh. I bit my lip and thrashed about on the bed, giving small moans and grunts until the orgasm rocked me, screaming and panting.

I gave one final shudder and fell back, out of breath and sweating profusely. The bed creaked again, and the mattress shifted, as if someone were moving next to me. When I reached over, though, there was nothing to feel.

"Don't go away," I begged the emptiness, "come back and let me see you, let me touch you."

"I will be back, Mara," he whispered, his deep echoing voice caused delicious chills to wash over me, "you will see and touch me soon. And I will leave you a gift, so you never need go to anyone else."

Then there was silence and I felt his departure as if it were physical pain. "No," I called to him, struggling to open my eyes, trying to reach out to him so that he wouldn't leave, "I don't want a gift. I want you. Don't go."

A loud thump in the hallway and the sound of a door closing somewhere woke me with a start. I opened my eyes to the sun that was streaming in through the studio windows and I could see that the painting was exactly as I had left it the previous afternoon. Apollo had no eyes, and only the mere suggestion of a body. "God," I said stretching and pulling myself out of bed, "that was really weird." Wrapping the sweat-soaked top sheet around me, I went down the stairs to see what had fallen to wake me up.

Directly inside the front door was a book and I bent down to pick it up. It was a copy of Bullfinch's *The Age of Fable*, an old book, but in perfect condition, beautifully bound in black leather with gold leaf titles. I carried it up the stairs and sat down in an armchair to look at it closer.

Opening the cover, I was surprised to discover that it was a first edition, more surprised still to see my name inscribed on the flyleaf. "To Mara Hawthorne," it read, "a woman belonging to a different age." There was no signature, but I knew the only person who could have given it to me was Jonathan Weber. He was also, curiously enough, the only person who could have unlocked my front door. I felt flattered at the value of the book and his generosity. I laughed to myself. What the hell would he have given me if I had slept with him? Then again, at the same time, I was annoyed that he felt free enough to enter my apartment without my permission.

"So," I said, opening the first page and beginning to read, "I'll just let him stew a while before I thank him."

It was well after twelve when I closed the book. My stomach was empty and hollow; I realized that I hadn't eaten since last night. Not only that, I hadn't been grocery shopping since I arrived and there was no food in the apartment. When I got up from the chair, I realized how exhausted I was. The bed, even disheveled as it was, looked so very tempting. What I really needed was a nice, long nap, but I forced myself to get dressed and go out.

When I went outside, I saw that it was raining lightly. That, plus the difficulties of carrying bags of groceries back with me, made me decide to take my car, even though the closest food store was only a few blocks away. Stopping at the bank first, I opened a local account and ordered a debit card and a set of checks. When I finally made it to the food store it was around one-thirty. Pushing the cart down the aisles half-heartedly, I finally picked up enough to keep me going for at least a month. Although I did buy some fresh fruit and vegetables, most of the food I bought was junk: pre-prepared meals, frozen dinners, and microwave entrees for one. I'd never been much of a cook and when I was painting I liked something quick and easy.

The cashier was, I thought, overly friendly, a buxom, middle-aged brown-haired woman who liked to talk. Unfortunately, I'd always had a certain waif-like quality that seemed to bring out the worst in these matronly types. But I smiled and made the appropriate responses to her questions, because the name on her tag was the same as my mother's.

"You're new around here, aren't you, honey?"

"Yes," I admitted, "I just moved in yesterday."

"Not a student, are you?" She gave me a long appraising glance, then shook her head without giving me a chance to respond. "Nope, you don't look like a student. Where are you staying?"

"I have a third floor apartment over on Pine Street."

Her hand seemed to hesitate over the price reader. "Not the Weber house, is it?" It seemed ridiculous, but her voice sounded pitched higher as she said it.

I nodded, "Yes, it's very nice. Jonathan has just redecorated the place. Has he owned it long?"

"Been in his family ever since I can remember. It was his idea to turn it into apartments, though. Said it was too big for a bachelor." She bagged and totaled my order and I handed her cash.

She chuckled. "We don't see much of the green stuff these days. We do take credit if you'd prefer."

"Nope, cash is good with me." I'd had to cancel all my accounts to keep them safe from my ex's attentions. "I just opened my bank account and don't have my checks or my debit card yet."

She nodded. "In that case would you like to fill out a check-cashing card for next time, honey?" She opened the cash register drawer and counted out my change. "That makes it easier for you than carrying around a lot of money."

I didn't really care, but she seemed so eager to help that I agreed. "That would be nice, thank you."

She turned the key in her register. "I'll just pick one up for you over at the office. Be back in a sec."

I spent the time studying the stand of papers next to me. I laughed at some of the stories covered, especially the one about the alien advising the president. Damn, I thought, vampires, alien invasions, half-wolf babies, haunted houses, - people will believe almost anything.

"You want one of those, honey?" The cashier's voice brought me out of my thoughts, "I can add it on, if you like."

"No," I said with a half-grin, "but I'll take a local paper if you have one."

She pulled one off the stack at the end of her register and placed it on top of the filled bags in my cart. "That'll be fifty cents and here's the form for the card. Why don't you fill it out now, since we aren't busy and you can pay by check next time you stop."

I handed her two quarters from the change she'd given me earlier and started to fill out the card. She leaned over the counter, watching me intently. "You live alone?"

I was beginning to get annoyed at her prying. "Well, unless you count Owen Culver as company, I guess I do."

This time there was no questioning her reaction. She stiffened slightly, looked around almost guiltily, and gave a small nervous laugh. "Owen Culver?" She whispered the name as if it were an obscenity. "I haven't heard that name in years. Have you seen him?"

"No, I haven't seen him. I was only joking." I handed her the paper. "Thank you. I guess I'll be seeing you around."

I started to push the cart out the door when I felt a hand on my shoulder. "Mara," she must have read my name on the form. Her voice was low and earnest, and she followed me out to my car, lightly putting her hand on my arm. "Owen Culver is nothing to joke about. Tell that Jonathan Weber you want out of your lease and move somewhere else. A little thing like you, all on your own, in that house, why, honey, it just gives me the chills. Move out."

I didn't say anything, but shut the lid of the trunk on the groceries I had been unloading while she talked. My stomach rolled; I was tired, hungry and in no mood to argue with a total stranger about my choice of living quarters. "Thank you again," I said, a note of finality in my voice, and put the car keys into my purse. "I'll think about it."

"Well then, you take care," she called after me. I crossed the street and approached the pizza place Jonathan had pointed out last night. Before I entered I looked back and the cashier was still standing there staring after me. In spite of the fact that I felt slightly nauseous and my legs were wobbly, I gave her a bright smile and waved. She nodded her head. "Remember what I told you," she called to me and went back into the store.

I went into the pizza parlor grinning to myself. People will believe anything.

The place was empty, although used plates and napkins were strewn about several of the tables. Checking my watch I realized that it was too late for lunch and too early for dinner. I stood waiting for a few minutes and when no one appeared to take my order, I rang the bell on the counter.

"Be right there," a young female voice called out from the back, and the girl who had spoken to Jonathan last night in the diner walked out. She seemed less weepy today and although I could tell she recognized me, she didn't smile. In fact, she came as close to not acknowledging my presence as was possible in the situation.

"Hi," I said, "Susan, isn't it?"

"Yeah," she said sullenly, "what do you want?"

I looked up at the menu, "I'll have a small, with extra cheese, bacon, pepperoni, and green peppers. And a large cola."

She rang up my food and when I paid, she pointed to the seating area. "Take a booth; I'll bring it out when it's ready."

I chose the cleanest table and sat down. A radio was playing in the back of the store and I closed my eyes, lightly tapping my fingers to the song's rhythm. I was so tired; my head drooped and I pulled it back, attempting to shake off the strange exhaustion that overcame me.

The next thing I knew, a teenaged boy I hadn't seen before set my pizza and drink on the table.

"You okay, lady?"

"Yeah," I said, rubbing my forehead and eyes, "I guess I just nodded off. Where's Susan?"

"She had an appointment." He shrugged. "You want anything else?"

"No, this'll be fine, thanks."

Eating revived my energy slightly and I managed to finish all but one piece of pizza. After drinking the soda, I felt awake enough for the drive back home. I thought about taking the last piece home for later, but when I stood up I felt as if I was going to be sick. I threw a few dollars on the table for a tip and rushed out.

By the time I crossed the street to my car the wave of nausea passed. Nevertheless, I drove home with the window open. The cool rain on my face made me feel clean and refreshed, but when I arrived at my apartment, I was soaked and chilled. I swore as I got out of the car realizing I still had to get six bags of groceries up the stairs and put them away. And I was so tired.

"Jesus," I said, balancing two bags of frozen food, turning the key in my lock and kicking the door open, "it's not as if I didn't sleep last night. This is crazy." I dumped the bags on the landing and went back down for another load.

The rest of the bags were too heavy to carry more than one at a time. Finally, after what seemed countless trips up and down the stairs, I dragged the last bag from the trunk and slammed the lid down. A car pulled up behind me and honked its horn. I spun around and the bag broke open, spilling cans and bottles onto the sidewalk.

"Shit," I looked at the mess at my feet, leaned up against my car, and began to cry.

Jonathan Weber was out of his car in a second, wrapping an arm around my shoulders, and apologizing. "Oh, God, Mara, I'm so sorry, I didn't think you'd drop it."

"I didn't drop it," I squeezed the words out between sobs, "the goddamned thing broke."

He patted my shoulder, "Are you crying?"

I choked a bit and nodded my head.

"Aw, don't cry, Mara, I'll collect it all for you and bring it up. You're sopping wet, you go on and get dry, and I'll be along in a minute."

"Thank you." I dragged myself up the stairs for what I hoped would be the last time that day. I tripped over the bags that I'd left on the landing, swore again, and went into the bathroom. Leaving my clothes in a sodden heap in the tub, I wrapped myself in a towel, and walked out of the bathroom, just as Jonathan came in the front door.

He stopped and stared at me for a minute before averting his eyes. "I'm sorry again," he said, the expression I had caught in his eyes indicated he was anything but sorry to catch me practically naked. "You go change and I'll put some of this stuff away for you."

"Fine," I said, in a tone more biting than I intended, "just come on in and make yourself at home." Then I stalked over to the bedroom alcove and pulled the curtains. The bed was even more inviting than it'd been before I left and I wanted nothing more than to crawl into it and pull the covers over my head. "But no," I said quietly, nastily, "now I have to entertain my landlord."

"Did you say something?" Jonathan called.

"No, not really." I knew none of this was Jonathan's fault, he was actually trying to help, so I made an effort to respond cheerfully. "Oh, Jonathan, put the kettle on while you're at it and we'll have a cup of tea or something after I'm dressed."

"Good idea." Jonathan's voice was enthusiastic, eager.

I smiled to myself, while I pulled a pair of jeans and a sweater from my dresser. It's likely he's more interested in the 'or something' than the tea, Mara, so you go easy. As I started to slide the jeans up my legs, I noticed that the skin on my legs and thighs was discolored with angry looking red streaks. I sat down on the bed and touched the marks tentatively. The skin wasn't broken and the marks weren't painful. Shaking my head, I rubbed my legs once more, then lay back on the bed and stared at the ceiling...

"Mara? Are you okay?" Jonathan's voice woke me and I sat up quickly.

"Fine," I called and got up from the bed and finished dressing.

Sliding out from behind the curtains, I went to the bathroom and picked up a dry towel. "You sure were right about the rain," I admitted as I walked into the kitchen, rubbing my wet hair. "Do you think it will stop soon?"

I wondered how long I had been asleep. There was no sign of the groceries I'd bought and I assumed Jonathan had put them away for me. Now he was standing at the sink, washing some fruit. He chuckled and made a show of looking at the clock. "Oh, it'll probably stop in about three or four weeks. We're in the rain belt, you know."

"Oh." I sat down at the kitchen table and watched him for a while. He found a bowl and put the fruit into it, then sat it down in front of me.

"Here," he said graciously, as if we were in his apartment instead of mine, "have something to eat. You'll feel better. The water should be hot, soon." He went over to the stove and shook the kettle. "Here we go," he said as it whistled, "just what the doctor ordered." He filled the two mugs he had prepared and put them on the table along with two spoons, the sugar bowl, and a small container of milk.

I dipped the tea bag up and down, distractedly. "You know, Jonathan," I said as he sat down across from me, "you don't need to wait on me. I can take care of myself."

"Yeah," he said, "I'm sure you can. But you just looked so down, so tired, I thought I should help you out a bit."

"Well," I poured some milk into my tea and took a sip, "thank you. I appreciate it. Just don't...." Don't make a habit of it was what I wanted to say, but he looked so sincere, so boyish, that I softened the thought. "Just don't spoil me too much."

"So, how'd you sleep last night?"

"What?"

"You know, with the storm and all. Did you lay awake all night listening to the rain?"

"No," I felt a slow blush creep up my neck, recalling the dream, "I slept great. I don't even remember hearing the rain."

"That's good. I see you were even prepared for the electricity going out," he waved an arm around, "all these candles. You were better off than I was, I just stumbled around, cursing the darkness."

"You should've called," I said without thinking, "I would've given you some." I blushed again, realizing that, given our circumstances last night, what I said was a double-entendre. "You know, candles."

He had the good grace not to refer to my slip. "I might have done that, but the phones were out too. And, you gave me the distinct impression you wanted to be alone."

"Well," I said with a tired smile, "there's that."

An uncomfortable silence fell over us. I sipped my tea and closed my eyes to think. Now was probably the time to thank him for the book, but I still resented his intrusion and didn't want him to get the idea he could walk in at any time. I came here to paint, I reminded myself again, not to carry on an affair with my landlord.

"Well," Jonathan's voice sounded slightly harsh interposed on the quiet sound of the rain hitting the roof, "aren't you even going to ask?"

I lifted my head up and opened my eyes with great effort. I had almost nodded off again. "Ask about what?"

"Owen Culver."

"Oh," I said with a small laugh, "him again. He's getting to be quite the topic of conversation."

"Why? Who have you been talking to?" Jonathan seemed angry that I might've heard the story from someone else.

I laughed again. "The cashier in the grocery store, for one. Although she didn't really have much to say about him, she just told me to break my lease and move out. But she did give me the feeling that I might as well move in with Satan himself as live here. What was he, anyway? Some sort of ax murderer?"

"Owen? God, no, he was nothing that horrible. For a man of his time, I suspect he was quite a hell-raiser, but in a totally different way. According to all reports, he was a heartless philanderer."

I chuckled as I got up and put the heat under the tea kettle again. "And for that he's doomed to haunt my apartment forever? Seems to me he's gotten a bad rap. Although," I took an apple from the bowl and bit into it, leaning back on the counter, "considering my luck with men, it figures I would move into the situation."

"Your luck with men—why should you say that?" Jonathan's voice was sharp, offended.

I gave him a quick glance, "I have a notorious habit of picking the worst possible partner. But I don't really want to discuss any of that. So what happened to Owen Culver that he should still be around?"

"Well," Jonathan lowered his voice slightly and looked around, "he was murdered."

"Really?" I had a feeling I knew what Jonathan was leading up to and surprisingly it didn't bother me. But I played the game as expected. "Where?"

"I don't want to alarm you, but they found his body here, over in your studio. The father of a girl he had gotten pregnant shot him twice, once in the heart, and once in the genitals. They say it took years to get the blood stain out of the floor, and that every year on the anniversary of his death it comes back."

I tried to put the proper expression of fear and loathing on my face but didn't quite succeed. Finally, much to Jonathan's surprise, I burst out in hysterical laughter. The harder I tried to control my reaction, the funnier the situation seemed. Tears streamed down my face and my stomach started to ache.

"It's true," he said indignantly. I could tell that he didn't know how to respond, that my laughter really threw him off balance. "And I don't see what's so funny. Owen Culver was my great-great-grandmother's brother, and I swear this is all true."

"And now I'm supposed to swoon into your arms in fear, right?" I smirked at him, not unkindly, then chuckled and shook my head. "So tell me, Jonathan, does this story usually work for you?"

"Well," he gave me the innocent, boyish smile of his that I found so endearing, "it doesn't hurt most of the time. Not going to buy it, are you?"

"No, not this time. No offense, okay?"

"Okay. But tell me the truth, aren't you even the slightest bit frightened, knowing the awful facts of Uncle Owen?"

"Jesus, Jonathan, I lived ten years in New York and not always in the best of areas. People got shot all the time, although," and I giggled again irreverently, "not always in such an appropriate spot. Poor Owen, I said before he'd gotten a bad rap and now I know it's true. Knowing the truth, as you put it, doesn't frighten me. If anything, it's probably made me more sympathetic toward him." The teakettle whistled and I filled my cup again. "That is, it would if I believed in him. So, when's his anniversary? I'll look out for the stain and call the papers if it appears."

Jonathan gave me an odd look, and I got the impression that he was more spooked than he let on. "Actually, it's in two weeks. You might want to arrange to be somewhere else at the time. You know, just in case."

I smiled at him. "Your place, for instance?"

Jonathan shrugged, "Well, you'd be more than welcome, then or any other time, for that matter."

"I'll be sure to remember that," I said dryly.

He got up from the table and stood in front of me. "I guess I'd better be going, then. I still have a stack of papers to grade from the other night." Awkwardly, he bent toward me to give me a kiss.

His lips never made it to mine. A crash from the studio made him jump and turn around. "What the hell was that?"

The canvases that I had stacked in the corner had fallen over, narrowly missing my current painting. I walked over and set them upright again. "You know, Jonathan, if you're so jumpy about this place, you probably shouldn't be telling ghost stories."

"It's not that," he said sharply, "the noise startled me, that's all." He moved across the room and looked at the canvas I had started. "Is this your new one?"

I nodded, slightly embarrassed. I didn't like people evaluating my work until it was completed, if then. Suddenly, inexplicably angry, I stood with my arms crossed, as if daring him to make a comment, any comment, while we both studied the painting.

"Daphne and Apollo," was all he said. Then his lips brushed my cheek delicately. "I'll see you later, I hope." He was halfway down the stairs when I pulled my attention from the unfinished canvas long enough to realize that he'd left.

"Yeah," I called to him, not taking my gaze from the nebulous figures that danced in front of me, pleading with imagined eyes and hands for the life my paint would impart, "later." Before the front door had even closed, I was taking off my sweater, my jeans, and pulling a brush out of the can. Thoughts of Jonathan Weber and Owen Culver, of erotic dreams and philandering ghosts, faded into nothing as the work completely possessed my mind.

By six o'clock the next morning I had done as much painting as was physically possible for me at one time. I'd been at it for over fourteen hours; my legs ached, my arms trembled and my spine felt as if it had been tied into a thousand knots. But none of that mattered since the figures of Apollo and Daphne had been given life and form.

The smooth skin of Daphne's thighs and stomach was overlaid with the rough gnarls of bark, her wind-blown hair becoming tendrils, green and growing, her outstretched arms sprouting the stubs of limbs and branches. Small beads of sap and blood and sweat dappled her virginal breasts; the exhilaration of the chase seemed to drain from her face as she realized the fate to which she had condemned herself. A slight twist to her mouth suggested that perhaps she now regretted her hasty prayer for salvation.

"Too late, babe," I addressed her, my hands on my hips, "Didn't anyone ever tell you that it's better to be a ravished nymph than a virgin tree? Anyway," my gaze now went to the figure of Apollo, "how could you resist him?"

Even to my usually self-critical eyes, the Apollo was magnificent. He had come up behind her, catching her by the tiny waist, twisting her around to accept his embrace. From one hand fluttered the garment he had ripped from the nymph's body, the other hand grasped the skin soon to be bark with long, sensuous fingers. The muscles of his chest glistened with sweat and his face glowed with passion. He was completely naked and his penis was startlingly erect.

I shivered; the portrayal of Daphne was good, I knew, as good as or perhaps slightly better than most of my paintings. But the figure of Apollo frightened me, he was so shockingly lifelike. I ached to put my hand on his chest, to draw him to me, to fall with him to the forest floor and make love there beneath the branches of the woman who'd denied him.

"She didn't love you," I said with only half a smile for my foolishness, "but I do. I would stay with you forever."

I stood, swaying in front of the canvas for a long time, caught up in the spell of the story and the spell of his eyes. Have you come from my brush or from the longings of my soul? I could hardly remember painting him; he seemed the culmination of my dreams, not just the ones I'd experienced here, but all my dreams and fantasies. If only you were real, I thought and felt tears of despair streaming down my face.

The sound of a toilet flushing in the apartment downstairs finally brought me back to reality with a start. I shook myself and went into the shower, wiping my eyes and laughing. "Jesus, Mara, you've been working too long."

After I'd dried off, I realized that I was too keyed up to sleep; the exhaustion of the day before was gone in face of the exhilaration of my creation. I dressed in my last pair of clean jeans and an oversized t-shirt, rummaged through the closet for my raincoat, picked up my keys and went down the stairs.

The morning sun was pale and shrouded with clouds, but the air was clean. I felt that I could almost see the growth of the grass and the early spring flowers bursting through the sodden earth. Walking slowly as if in a trance, I went around the block, touching each tree I saw in a ritual homage.

I passed Jonathan's porch and headed for my side stairway, when I heard my name called and turned around. He was sitting on a chair, his feet propped up on the railing next to a steaming mug. He folded the paper he'd been reading, dropped it on the porch, and stood up.

"Good morning, Mara. You're up early, aren't you? I thought you artists slept late."

He hadn't shaved, and the flannel shirt he wore was unbuttoned. I stared at him as if I'd never seen him before and suddenly realized that Jonathan bore an arresting resemblance to my Apollo. Maybe it was the set of his jaw, the musculature of his chest, or just the way his eyes looked at me, with passion and promise. Whatever it was, I wanted to throw myself onto him and rip the clothes from his body to see if the rest of him matched the god who waited for me upstairs. Instead, I put my hands into my pockets and blushed.

"Actually," I said quietly, not daring to move, "I haven't been to bed. Yet." The last word lingered in the air like an invitation.

"Well then," he said with a broad smile, his teeth flashing white against his unshaven face, "maybe you'd like to come in for a cup of coffee."

I nodded, not trusting my voice. He came down the few steps and wrapped his arm around my waist, pulling me to him.

Once we were inside, he shut the door and locked it. I could feel the click of the latch deep within me and my pulse raced. Jonathan reached over and took my hands in his, smiling down into my face. "You really didn't come here for coffee, did you?"

I wanted to insist that I did, but my trembling hands betrayed me. "No," I admitted, my voice a frightened whisper, "I came for you."

"That's what I hoped."

Jonathan didn't waste any time; he scooped me up, carried me back to his bedroom and gently deposited me onto his enormous bed. It was still unmade, and the covers were thrown back to reveal black satin sheets. It did not seem like a bed designed for sleep, it was designed instead for seduction. He loomed over me, the smile I'd found so charming now seemed merely arrogant and the hands that removed my jeans and my panties were so expert, so practiced that I began to doubt that this was what I really wanted.

But at least he's real, Mara, I thought, my eyes darting about trying to focus on anything but his face, and his now naked body, he's not a dream or a dead god on canvas. He's live and tangible and here.

The thought reassured me and I gave him a quavering smile as he removed my shirt. Soon I lay naked in front of him.

"Mara," he said, but the voice was not the one I wanted to hear, "I feel like I've known you forever, like I've waited forever for you." He lay down next to me, his hands busy, touching and stroking my breasts. His mouth nibbled at my neck, murmuring endearments, urging me to relax, to let him love me. My body responded to him fully, but my mind was somewhere else. And although I tried to ignore where it took me, I knew the location with certainty: two flights up in a fragrant bower that existed only in my imagination.

When Jonathan finally entered me, I made the appropriate responses, my moans and cries joining his, my traitor body moving to his thrusts and pounding. He ducked his head to suck at my nipples, saying my name over and over and I arched my back to meet him. He began to grunt, screaming his pleasure, his release and his frenzied pulsing brought me quickly to orgasm.

He rolled from me with a sigh that I echoed and he misunderstood. "Yeah," he said, reaching for a tissue to remove the condom I hadn't even realized he'd used, "I agree, that was incredible." He kissed me on the forehead then sat up. "But unfortunately, I have a class in about," he looked at a bedside clock, "oh, forty-five minutes, so I have to go." I turned my head and sighed again, feeling tears well up in my eyes. Jonathan did not notice, instead he left the room and went straight to the shower.

By the time he returned, I'd gotten control of my emotions and my disappointment. Of course it was nothing like your dreams, you silly girl, I thought scathingly, what on earth could be? Two weeks ago I would've been ecstatic over the sex. Jonathan was a good lover, an interesting person and he seemed to be crazy about me. There was absolutely no reason for me to be disappointed.

I watched him furtively as he dressed; he had a nice body, not as muscular nor as massive as the painting, but certainly nothing to be ashamed of. When he finished tying his tie and selecting a suit coat, he came over and sat next to me on the bed, giving the side of my hip a gentle slap.

"I'm so sorry I have to rush away, but why don't you just stay here and get some sleep? Make yourself at home; have some coffee or breakfast or whatever. And remember," he smiled and brushed back my hair where it had fallen, partially covering my breasts, "that I won't mind at all if you're still here when I get back."

I listened to his footsteps until the front door closed. Then I pulled the black satin sheet over me, rolled to my side and fell fast asleep.

When I woke, I was confused to hear Jonathan speaking. I knew he'd left and hadn't heard the door open, so he couldn't be back. I pulled on my t-shirt and followed the sound of his voice. When I got to the kitchen, I understood as I heard, "So if you'll leave your name, your number and a brief message, I'll call you right back."

I laughed, poured myself a cup of coffee and went to turn the volume down on his machine. Although he'd invited me and obviously wanted me to stay, that didn't entitle me to listen in on his messages. But the urgency of the caller's voice stopped my hand and I sat down at the kitchen table with a flop when I recognized her voice.

"Hi, uh, Jonathan, it's me." It was Susan, the girl from the diner and the pizza place. "I took the test this morning and it was positive." She paused and I could hear the tears in her voice. "And you know how you said last night that you would take care of me, if I were, well, you know." She blew her nose and continued, "Well, I am." A long pause ensued. "Oh, God, Jonathan, I'm pregnant." After finally breaking the bad news her words began to flow so fast I almost had difficulty following them.

"And you know it's yours, there's never been anyone else, and I love you and you said last night that you loved me and that you would take care of me. And last night was so wonderful, you know, and I'm sorry I was so mad about you being out with that woman, I know you don't like her, she's too old for you, that's what you said and you just took her out to dinner because you felt sorry that she was all alone. And, well anyway, I wanted you to know that I do understand and I feel better and I know you'll take care of me. Call me when you get home and I can come over again tonight." Susan paused again, then repeated in a plaintive voice, "I love you. Call me."

I sat quietly for a few seconds listening to the tape on the answering machine click back into place. I took a sip of the coffee, it was too strong, too bitter. Flinging the mug as hard as I could, I delighted in the crashing of the pieces as they shattered and fell down to the floor beneath the phone.

That goddamned son of a bitch. I kept repeating it over and over as I dressed. That goddamned son of a bitch. "Waited forever for me, huh?" I addressed his bed as if it were him, "'And last night was so wonderful,'" I mimicked, "Jesus, Jonathan, last night? Your bed hardly even cooled off from Susan before you eased me into it." That goddamned son of a bitch. "Well, since this 'woman' is too old for you, someone you just feel sorry for, I can promise you it'll be a cold day in hell before I get in here with you again." Angrily, I ripped the black satin sheets completely off the bed, rolled them up into a crumpled ball, and threw them into the corner of the room.

That goddamned son of a bitch.

I slammed his front door and stormed up the stairs to my apartment, taking my shoes off and kicking them clear across the room. I stopped in front of my canvas just long enough to throw a drop cloth over it, "And I don't need you looking at me again while I'm sleeping. You're the one that got me into this in the first place; standing there so goddamned sexy, making me want someone, looking just enough like him to make it happen."

I crawled into bed, still ranting at the covered painting, knowing that eventually my anger would run its course and I would be fine. "You're all the same, every stinking one of you, you can't keep your dicks inside your pants long enough to stay out of trouble. Even poor Owen couldn't keep his hands off the ladies to save his life. I swear if I had a gun, I'd shoot the genitals off every man I meet, before they can hurt me." With that last vindictive statement my rage ran out; I wiped the tears from my face, pulled the covers up over my still clothed body and fell asleep.

I slept until late that afternoon, dreamlessly. Maybe my anger kept the erotic dreams away, maybe since I'd just had a living man my subconscious decided that I didn't need a dream lover, or maybe just covering the painting removed the influence on my overly active imagination. Whatever the reason, the undisturbed rest was exactly what I needed, and when I woke up I felt revitalized, able to look at the situation with Jonathan in a different light.

I remembered my anger of this morning almost sheepishly. It wasn't as if Jonathan had pledged his eternal love to me. It wasn't as if we meant anything more to each other than just plain sex. No promises had been made between us, it was not my trust he had betrayed. I felt sorrier for Susan now than I did for myself. "But now's as good a time as any, sweetie, to learn how the world works. That's what college is for."

I showered to wash Jonathan's touch from my body. There was still anger, I realized, but now I knew that most of it was directed at myself for allowing this to happen. "Never again," I said as I got out of the shower and looked at my reflection in the mirror. "Never again." I brushed my teeth, dried my hair and dressed in the jeans I had worn that morning, but dropped my t-shirt in the hamper.

Putting my hand to the knob of the bathroom door, I gave a self-depreciating laugh, "So how about it, Owen? From now on it'll just be you and me, two lost souls together." I snorted, "After all, love's never done much for either of us, has it?"

When I opened the door, I was unprepared for the blast of cold air that met me. I shivered and went to the radiator, adjusting the knob, but nothing happened. "Dammit," I swore, "I need some heat. It's as cold as a stinking tomb in here." I crossed my arms over my naked chest. "Come on, baby," I urged the radiator, "Give your friend Mara a little heat." It sighed and sputtered and gave off one more gush of cold before the heat filtered through. "Thank you."

I went to the closet and found one of my painting shirts still clean; buttoning it up, I thought that tomorrow I would have to find a laundromat. "But that's tomorrow," I went into the kitchen and pulled a prepared dinner from the freezer, "we still have to get through tonight."

When I'd finished the meal, I dumped the tray into the wastebasket and put my fork into the sink. I didn't feel much like painting, didn't own a television, didn't know anyone to call on the phone. It promised to be a long evening. I heard an odd fluttering outside my front door, but when I looked out the studio window, I saw that the wind was blowing hard again and more rain had started.

I went back to the kitchen and poured myself a large glass of scotch, tuned my clock radio to the college station and sat back in an armchair. "Well, Owen," I realized that talking to a non-existent ghost was probably worse than talking to yourself, but what the hell, I was an artist and entitled to my eccentricities, "what's on the agenda for tonight? Maybe we should just sit around here and tell each other the dismal stories of our love lives." I refilled my glass and wandered about the apartment, ending up at the radiator, giving the knob one more twist.

"Ahhraa," it moaned at me.

"Not much of a conversationalist, are you?" I laughed, slightly drunk. "God, this is boring; I wish something would happen, I don't care what."

As I spoke, three things happened simultaneously. Lightning flashed, the lights went out and there was someone pounding on my front door. "Hold on a minute," I called to the person at the door, "my lights just went out." I lit one of the candles I'd used the previous night and walked down the stairs, opening the door to a wet and bedraggled Jonathan Weber. He gave me a twisted, sheepish grin, and extended his fist to me, offering about a dozen wilted roses in his fist.

"Hi," his voice was uncertain, "can I come in?"

"I don't think so," I said sternly.

"Just to talk, please."

"I can't think what we'd have to talk about, Jonathan. What happened this morning was a mistake from the beginning. I don't intend for it ever to happen again."

"I won't try anything, I promise," he smiled at me, his face seemed so sincere, so innocent, "I just want to explain. I think I have to explain."

"And that's an admirable sentiment, Jonathan. But you don't owe me an explanation. Just go home."

I tried to slam the door on his face, but he blocked the door with his body and pushed his way through. Closing the door behind him, he dropped the roses onto the floor of the landing and reached out to grab my shoulders. "Please, Mara, at least talk to me. I'll only stay a few minutes, I promise."

"Okay, but take your hands off me."

He let my shoulders go reluctantly and I darted up the steps before him. I went into the kitchen, put the candle on the table, and set my hand-wound timer.

"What's that for?" Jonathan stood before me, offering the roses again.

"I give you fifteen minutes. You can have your say and then leave." I took the roses from him and put them into the sink. "These won't help you any, either. I'm not that much of an old-fashioned girl to swoon away at the sight of a dozen long-stemmed roses."

"But I just found them outside your door. I didn't buy them intending to...."

"Like hell you didn't." I crossed my arms in front of me and leaned back on the counter. "So, talk," I said, tapping my finger on the timer dial, "your time is running out."

Jonathan took a big gulp of air. "I wanted to explain about Susan. I know you must've heard her message." He laughed uneasily, "I found the remains of your coffee cup on the floor."

I didn't say a word. The ticking of the timer was almost deafening in the silence and the near darkness.

"Well, I'll admit that Susan and I had a brief affair, and she sort of latched on to me. I've tried to break it off many times, but she always comes back. This isn't the first time she's thought she was pregnant, it probably won't be the last. For her, that is, but not for me. I talked to her today and told her that we're through. I promise you. If she really is pregnant, well then I'll help her out the best I can. But I don't love her, I love you."

I stared at him for a long minute. "How convenient for you that fathers today don't carry shotguns; otherwise you might end up like your great uncle Owen."

The apartment seemed to grow colder and Jonathan shifted nervously on his feet. "That's not funny, Mara."

"It wasn't meant to be, Jonathan. Does philandering run in the family, or do you just feel it to be a male prerogative?"

"Please, Mara, don't be like this." His voice was low and persuasive and he managed to sound totally sincere. "I want to make it up to you and I will. This morning was special to me, you have to believe that, and if I'd been able to stay I would have told you all about Susan." He hung his head slightly. "I'm not proud of any of this, but I love you. Hell, I'm not perfect, no one is, but I'd like a second chance with you. Please."

He couldn't have seen my expression soften in the candlelight, but he must have felt it. The cold air between us felt almost electric, and when his arms came around me I leaned into him.

"One second chance," I said sternly. "One. That's all you'll get from me."

He kissed me. I shivered. Standing here in the darkness with the scent of the roses in the sink seemed so close to my dreams. But I could feel him, could touch him and I knew that he wouldn't vanish when I woke.

Jonathan lifted me up on the counter and struggled with my buttons. When he couldn't undo them fast enough, he swore and ripped the entire shirt open, his mouth fastening hungrily to my breast.

I jumped and pushed his head away from me, "Jesus, do you have to be so rough?"

He looked up at me and his face seemed brutal in the candlelight. "I want you so bad, Mara. I have to have you, right here, right now."

"And if I say no?" My voice trembled, his passion was frightening, overwhelming and I didn't want to be swept up in it.

"Then," he said, his hand closing tightly over the crotch of my jeans, "I'll take you anyway. You know you want me, just say it, say you want me, Mara."

He worked my zipper down and pulled my jeans and panties down to my knees, fumbling with his own pants and dropping them to the floor. He put his hands on the inner sides of my knees, and pushed them apart as he struggled to enter me.

"No," I said, shoving him away, "I don't want to, not like this. Please stop, you're scaring me."

His laugh was harsh, "How could I scare you? You're the one who's not afraid of anything, remember? And if you're not afraid of dead men, why should you be frightened by me? I won't hurt you," his rough hands on my body belied his statement, "I just want to love you."

"No." I said it so softly that he couldn't have heard. But it echoed off the walls of the apartment, roaring in my head. Jonathan stopped groping and lifted his head, listening. A great blast of frigid air hit us, making me shiver uncontrollably. He stared at me in shock for a minute.

"No," I whispered to him in the darkness and the word roared back at us. The dishes in the cabinets began to clatter, the doors shook open, and glasses and plates began to fall and shatter.

Jonathan backed off, hastily pulling up his pants, not even stopping long enough to zip them up. "I'd better go now," he said, viewing the wreckage on the floor with terror, his hands grasping the waist of his pants, "I'll call...."

"No."

This time I did not need to say it; someone else said it for me. I heard the door slam as Jonathan left and looked around at the kitchen. The shaking subsided and I watched one final glass fall, as if in slow motion, and break apart on the floor.

My shoulders heaved and I slid off the counter. I couldn't tell at first whether I was crying or laughing. But when the deep, thrilling voice I'd heard before in my dreams began to laugh, I joined him, stunned and more than slightly hysterical, until tears streamed down my face.

"I guess that showed him, Owen," I whispered when my spasms had passed. "Thank you." I expected some sort of response from my ghostly defender, but there was nothing. The room felt empty and lonely. At that very moment the timer went off. I hit it with my hand, gave a half smile. "And, ladies and gentlemen, time's up."

Almost a week passed with no word from Jonathan and no sign of the presence that once occupied my apartment. I felt strangely deserted by both of them. I could easily understand Jonathan's attitude, why he didn't want to face me or the wrath waiting for him in my apartment. But where had Owen gone? He had been here; that evening with Jonathan had proved it. But just as certainly I knew that he was here no longer.

Maybe his work was done, I thought, maybe he redeemed his soul by saving me from Jonathan. "But that's probably a load of bull. And you'll never know, Mara," I said aloud, "so just forget about it."

But I found that I couldn't forget. The erotic dreams stopped as did the inspiration I'd received for my painting. I grew despondent and moody until it was all I could do to drag myself out of bed. One afternoon, after spending long, frustrating hours trying to finish the Apollo and Daphne canvas, I threw down my brushes in anger and flung myself onto the bed.

"You said you'd never leave me, that we'd be together forever," I cried to my invisible lover, "and then you left." I buried my head in the pillow. "Come back," I begged the emptiness, "come back to me. I want you. I love you."

Suddenly a warm spring breeze blew through the apartment; my breath caught in my throat and my tears subsided. The prisms on the chandelier sang their crystal songs again and the fragrance of flowers was intoxicating. Chandelier? I thought, and flowers? Ah, relief flooded my body, the dream again.

But when I rolled over, I knew that I was not asleep. The apartment wasn't filled with flowers, the furniture was mine, and the overhead light had no prisms to jingle in the air. But still I heard them and smelled the roses. My eyes went to the painting of Apollo and

Daphne and once again the eyes of my canvas god met mine. I felt the thrill of his glance through my entire body, and when the figure moved and stepped off the canvas, I gasped. He laughed gently, and turned around to study the painting.

"A good likeness." His voice was deep, but slightly hollow at the same time, as if he was speaking to me from a long distance. "You have talent, my dear."

"Who are you?" My voice wavered slightly, this is not a dream, I reminded myself and my stomach tightened. I couldn't tell if it was fear or anticipation.

He turned back to me, and gave me a bow, graceful and courtly that did not seem incongruous even considering his lack of clothes. "You called and I came."

"Owen Culver?"

The movement of his head could have been a nod.

"But you're dead."

He didn't say anything, but crossed the room to me. His eyes burned on me and it became difficult for me to breath. It was as if he was draining the life from my body with his look. I knew he was and I didn't care. I reached up and unbuttoned my painting shirt, throwing it open and revealing my naked body to his stare. He smiled then, displaying teeth white and even. His cold hand reached down and delicately touched the skin of my stomach.

"Ah," I sighed and my body bucked slightly.

"You must ask me."

"Ask you?" I was confused at his hesitation. I wanted him so much. "Ask you what?"

"It is difficult for me to speak," the words fell slowly from his mouth, "I am sorry." He gave a small grimace then smiled again. "You must ask me to take you."

A flood of passion washed over my body, and a hot flush crept into my face. I hesitated for only a moment. "Yes," I whispered, shameless in my desire for him, "I want you. No one but you."

"Good." That one word from him was a vow, a promise and I knew deep in my soul that somehow my words had sealed a pact with him forever.

God help me, I thought as I studied the figure that hovered over me, I love him. And I don't care who or what he is.

Then he touched me again and my entire body seemed to explode into a blaze of desire. His mouth came down on mine, his lips were cold, but he kept them pressed to mine and I felt them grow warm. He was sucking the fire of my body into his. I wanted him to have it; there was nothing I would deny him.

I kept my eyes wide open, not wanting to miss the look of him. Everywhere his lips or his hands caressed, a small reddened patch would spring up, blossoming before my eyes like a delicate flower. There was no pain, only an excruciating ecstasy. I couldn't bear for it to continue and I couldn't bear for it to stop.

It might have been hours that I lay on the bed accepting his embraces and his icy kisses. Time, I knew, had no meaning for him and so it had no meaning for me. With mouth and tongue and hands, he explored every inch of my body. I grew so aroused that even the slightest touch anywhere would make me writhe and shudder. He didn't speak, he didn't need to. And I was long past speech.

I ached to touch him, to hold him tightly against me. Although with each passing minute, his limbs seemed to grow more substantial to my eyes and the weight of the body pressed to mine grew heavier, he was still out of reach, reminding me again and again that this was not a mortal man who held me in intimate embrace. Strangely, I was not frightened; this eeriness only intensified our lovemaking and his touch on me somehow became doubly precious because I could not return it.

And still his mouth and hands continued, coaxing me to the edge of despair, the brink of ecstasy. Finally, when I felt I could stand no more, he straddled me and gazed at me hungrily, his eyes blazing with the heat he had stolen from eager body.

"Yes," I breathed, reaching my arms up to him, feeling the contact of his body as no more than the delicate fingers of fog on naked skin.

He smiled, his fingers reached down and stoked my cheek gently. "Mara," he whispered and plunged into me, so desperately, so deeply. I screamed in excruciating pain. I never wanted it to end.

His penis was hard and unyielding like stone. Its invasion into the inferno of my vagina was an almost indescribable union of fire and ice, each element feeding the other endlessly. And it seemed endless. He withdrew and thrust repeatedly, and my body convulsed over and over, until my control broke down completely and I cried, writhing and shuddering, begging him to stop, begging him to never stop.

His thrusting grew more frenzied and as I watched, the outline of his ethereal body began to waver and dim. I could feel his moans start; a deep vibration that began in the very center of my being and echoed to my fingertips and my feet. My extremities hummed and buzzed with his pleasure and the hair on my head began to rise from the pillow and dance in the air.

Only when he exploded into me, did I finally close my eyes. As wild colors played behind my eyelids, I realized that I would die from his love. Not this time, perhaps, and not the next, but I would certainly die. And I realized too, regardless of this knowledge, that I would gladly give myself to him again.

His body collapsed on mine, crushing my bruised skin. I winced and smiled, feeling his breath touch my shoulder. When I opened my eyes he was not visible. But it no longer mattered; I was his forever. Even when I felt his presence depart, I knew he would return.

He did return, day after day, night after night, sometimes in dreams and sometimes during my waking hours. We did not make love again, and after several visits, I began to understand his limitations and the rules that governed his existence on this plane. He could speak, he could become visible, or he could exert his touch on living flesh. To manage all three at one time took tremendous effort and concentration.

I never knew how he would come to me, as a word breathed into my ear, a glimpse of his body out of the corner of my eye, or a gentle touch on my shoulder as I worked. Still, I knew he was with me and I was content.

"I would have you again."

I'd been putting the finishing touches on the Apollo canvas, when the words he breathed against my neck sent chills up my spine. My mouth twisted into a slow, sensual smile, I put my brush down and turned around only to be caught up in his invisible arms. "Hello, Owen," I said before his mouth covered mine.

He eased me down onto the floor of the studio and began to make love to me. His caresses were as intense and as unhurried as before, the only difference was that I could not see him. With my eyes closed, though, the remembered image of his face, his eyes, his magnificent body carried me deeper into frantic passion.

He entered me, I cried out in ecstasy. When my eyes flew open, they focused not on Owen, but on someone that should not have been there. I screamed again, this time in rage and fear. "Get out," I cried, still writhing under my lover. Owen's weight shifted on top of me, and I knew that he had turned his unseen eyes upon the face of the intruder.

"Get out," I screamed again, my voice hoarse, my throat aching.

Jonathan Weber stood over me, staring down unbelievingly at my shuddering body. I followed his gaze and saw my breasts flattened against an invisible chest, my pelvis rocked up and down violently on the tile floor by the thrusting of an invisible penis.

Jonathan's eyes opened wider, then he smiled, and began to unzip his pants, not understanding what he saw.

The blood in my veins turned to ice. Oh, God, I prayed, let him understand. Let him leave.

Owen continued his movements, more frantic and frenzied.

"Get out," I gasped between clenched teeth.

Jonathan laughed. "An interesting game, Mara," he said, slipping his pants off and idly stroking himself, "can two play?"

"Get out, you're not wanted here. Please, Jonathan, just leave now." Anything else I tried to say was lost in my final groans and the sounds of release that did not come from me. More than ever, I wanted to hold Owen to me, to prevent his anger. But as always he eluded my grasp and he pulled himself from me. I cried when I felt the pressure of his body lessen and disappear.

I met Jonathan's eyes, pleading with him. "Leave now, while you can. This isn't what you think, Jonathan, you don't understand."

"On the contrary, Mara," he said, lowering himself down on top of the body Owen had just left, "I understand quite well."

"No," I warned him. "Don't do this."

He laughed and shifted his weight so that he could enter me. I tried to scramble back away from him, but he grabbed my wrists and pinioned them to the floor. He smiled cruelly as he slammed into my already bruised body.

Suddenly the air in the apartment turned brutally cold and Jonathan began to choke.

I felt him wither inside me. His eyes were frantic with fear as his hands tried to loosen the invisible pressure on his neck. His body rose from mine. I quickly got up and ran to the corner of my bedroom, unable to believe what I saw.

Jonathan hung, suspended in mid-air, his legs kicking violently at something I knew he could not fight. His face paled and he coughed, bruises in the shape of long fingers appeared on his throat and his struggles grew less and less strenuous. Finally his limp body was flung across the room, where it hit the kitchen doorframe. Over my frightened sobs, I could hear the sharp crack of bones breaking, and Jonathan collapsed into an almost unrecognizable bundle of skin and bones. His staring eyes glazed over and blood gushed briefly from his nose and his mouth, his last breath visible in the frigid air. When it stopped, I was alone again, naked, bruised and screaming uncontrollably in the night.

So they put me here, where all I do is tell my story over and over again to doctors who merely nod, jotting endless notes on endless pages. They think I'm crazy; they think I'm a freak. It doesn't matter, nothing matters except for the fact that he's with me here, where no living man could ever enter. His promise to me, unlike all the others of my life, turned out to be true. He will never leave this plane of existence until I'm ready to leave with him.

I stroke my expanding stomach, softly, gently, knowing that it's the only touch I'll ever give to his child. That saddens me, I'd always wanted a baby. But Owen is beckoning to me, and when Owen calls for the last time, I'll go to him.

"Soon," I whisper to him across the room where he stands, watching and waiting. The doctors shake their heads and smirk at my supposed insanity. I merely smile, rocking back and forth on my chair. "I'll come soon, my love."

WITH THE WINGS OF ANGELS

We met for lunch at our favorite café. Late as usual, I approached her table, slightly out of breath, sat down and helped myself to a cup of coffee from the carafe she'd already ordered.

We didn't say a word to each other until after I'd finished the first cup of coffee. "Late night," she said without a trace of question in her voice.

"Yeah," I replied, "tell me about it."

Nan laughed. "I shouldn't have to—you were there after all."

"Well, I was there and yet I wasn't. Tell me how it looked to you."

"How it looked to me?" Nan shrugged, "You mean, how it looked like fun?"

I could tell she didn't know what I was asking. "No, tell me about it, as if it were a story. You know how I love your stories; you have the eyes and the soul of a poet."

"Oh." She poured herself and me another cup of coffee, closed her eyes for a second, cleared her throat and started to talk.

They came to my house together last night. I was surprised to see him in one way, and not at all in another. It was the first time I'd seen them together, although I knew all about them: her seemingly boundless passion for him, his apparent lack of commitment. God knows she and I'd been through it way too many times before, endlessly and in all its variations. With tears and with laughter, with despair and with hope, we'd analyzed the relationship, picking over details and motivations. Oh, there'd been others for her, of course, but he was the one to whom she constantly returned, in thought and deed.

And all of a sudden here he was, and with her. She kept her eyes down when she walked in the door and, in a quiet voice very much unlike her, informed me that the plans we'd made would stay the same, the three of us would attend the fetish club and view the scenes. She and I left him with a glass of wine, while we changed into our outfits for the evening. Mine was pure top, of course, all spandex and boots, a broad black belt with my rhino-hide whip tucked into the side. She was all in black, as usual. Black panties and front-close black lace bra, a tunic that buttoned down the front and a pair of leggings—her only concession to the club was a pair of black leather cuffs. The collar she'd planned on wearing was left behind. "He doesn't care for them," she confided. "And he doesn't really need it for control." Her breath caught in her throat. "At least not for me."

During the cab ride she was completely silent. It unnerved me; she'd never been quiet around me or others, she always chattered away, often aimlessly and at the slightest opportunity. But now it was just he and I, exchanging pleasantries about our business, the weather and his flight in. She sat between the two of us, ghostlike, staring straight ahead, biting at her lip slightly. At one point during our small talk, his hand brushed her thigh. A casual contact at best, but I felt her shiver beside me. And the emotion contained in that shiver said more than she ever could have.

I caught his eyes over her head and smiled. "It's really nice to see you," I said, aware I was beginning to repeat myself, chattering to make up for her silence. "Such a pleasant surprise."

"Is it?" He didn't smile. He looked down at her, then back at me. "I got an offer I couldn't refuse, so here I am."

I thought I might have caught a glimpse of tenderness in his eyes when he looked at her, but she shivered again and suddenly I wasn't so sure.

The club was not terribly crowded when we arrived. We settled in on a small couch, he and I. She stood uncertainly for a while in front of him and when he inclined his head, she knelt at his feet, an almost fluid fall, an effortless homage to his power as master. I motioned a waiter over to us, ordered for me and looked at him. He ordered a glass of wine for himself, then stroked her hair, lightly, absently. She moved into his touch like a cat, her eyes closed, her face oddly composed. "And the same for my slave. But only one."

The waiter brought the three glasses of wine. I was nervous, so I practically drained mine on the first taste. He sipped his slowly. We watched the activity in the club, small scenes were starting up here and there: two emaciated girls dressed in vinyl body suits took turns spanking an equally emaciated young man dressed in a schoolgirl uniform; a well- built middle-aged blonde wearing only stockings and a pair of stiletto-heeled pumps lay gagged, hogtied and writhing on an altar while black-robed men dripped hot wax on her back and ass; there were all possible variations of couples, trios and groups mingled in various stages and corners. Pretty much a typical night.

His eyes moved back and forth, taking it all in; the expression on his face was that of bored condescension. She focused completely on the floor in front of his feet.

Her wine sat untouched on the table until he deigned to notice her again. "Thirsty, little one? Tell me."

"Yes."

Just that one word. The only word I had heard her speak since we left my apartment. Amazing, I thought, how much can be contained within one word. She spoke it as if it were the summation of their entire relationship. Maybe it was. Maybe her one answer to him was always a yes, an unconditional acceptance of him, a constant welcome.

Nan's voice caught in her throat. I looked up at her and was surprised to see she was blushing. She didn't meet my gaze at all and her tone grew quieter. "It's strange," she confided, "so very strange what that one word did to me. My response was an instant and totally unexpected arousal." She laughed nervously. "And you, of all people, know that I don't care for other women, not in that way, not at all. I know her pretty well, probably as well as anyone. We've shared rooms, beds—hell, I've seen her naked more times than I can count. And she's always remained just a friend...."

As her voice trailed off, she poured the rest of the coffee, apportioning it evenly into our cups. She took a drink and started back in.

The whole situation was extremely exciting. Yes, it was frightening on many levels, but deeply arousing at the same time. "Thirsty, little one? Tell me."

"Yes."

He nodded to her. "Then drink. All of it."

She took the wine glass in both hands like a small child, looked up at him over the rim as if pledging his health and drank, her eyes never leaving his face. When it was empty she set it back down on the table. The club was noisy, so I wasn't entirely sure, but she might have sighed.

Then he stood up so abruptly that he startled me. He reached down, took her arm and pulled her up to him. "Ready?"

This time, the shiver that ran up and down her body was plainly visible. "Yes."

He led her to a cross post not too far from where we'd been sitting, not in full view of the entire club, but not completely out of the way either. Fastening each of her cuffs to the short chains at the ends of the post, he stood back for a minute, as if admiring his handiwork. He shook his head and removed a red silk scarf from his pocket, bent down and tied her ankles to the base. She stood quietly through all of this, totally obedient, with her arms held outstretched, her face as expressionless as his had been earlier. A casual observer would have thought that this was standard practice for her, being restrained in full view of a room full of strangers, at the mercy of this man. I knew, in fact, that this was her first time. That knowledge enhanced my excitement, I was witness to an intimate virgin encounter. I longed to experience it myself and knew that somewhere in the club there'd be a man who would bear the marks of my whip that evening. But I would not go off in search of him now; instead I was riveted to the sight of her.

He unbuttoned her tunic, excruciatingly slow in his motions, as if reluctant to expose her to the gaze of others. When he finished he peeled it from her, tucked it between her back and the wood of the post, then unfastened her bra and pushed that aside as well. Her skin was so pale, so totally white that it seemed to glow against the black of her sleeves and her leggings and the wood against which she was pressed. Her breasts were fuller than most, her nipples erect and slightly puckered in the open air. I felt my own tighten in response.

The club seemed to grow hotter and a small crowd began to gather around them. After all, they'd had never been seen here before and thus were a novelty, a new amusement for the jaded. He stood back not moving, just looking at her. Doms of both sexes came by and offered suggestions, hinting at permission to play, since it seemed he didn't want to. He just shook his head and turned them away. Eventually most of the crowd left—the scene before them seemed static, boring. Nothing remarkable about a bound half-naked woman and if things improved they could always come back.

Finally he approached her, warily as if she were a threat to him. Her eyes never left his face as he began to run his hands over her body. Lightly at first, and then roughly, he pinched and pulled at breasts and nipples until her pale skin began to redden and bruise. He pulled her leggings down to her knees and his hands kneaded her thighs, her skin warming and blushing to his touch. But not her face, her face remained as pale as death. Even when he roughly inserted his finger into her, she stayed expressionless. Unaffected.

He dropped his hands and moved his face closer to hers. Her lips moved, but I couldn't make out what she whispered to him from the cross. Asking him to give up, perhaps, or maybe berating him for his lack of action. Whatever she said, it hit its mark and drew an almost instantaneous reprisal.

He pulled away from her quickly and removed the belt from his tight-fitting jeans. The snap of leather rang through the club. You could see the fury in the way he moved, the tightness of his mouth, the tautness in the muscles of his arms. His first few strokes were tentative, testing her and him. But he was skilled and she was helpless and after a while he removed his own shirt and his whipping gained a purpose, a determination. Welts began to rise on her breasts and thighs from his attentions. The crowd that had wandered away came back and encouraged him with an approving murmur.

I knew that she was hurting; damn it, she had to have felt it. Tears flowed from her eyes and dripped onto her breasts, dripped on to him, mingling with his sweat. But her face showed no pain, no discomfort. Instead with each new stroke of his belt, she smiled. She closed her eyes and smiled, for God's sake. Smiled as if she was being caressed with the wings of angels.

And I thought to myself, if only I could smile like that, I would take the blows. Or if I could inspire that smile, I would gladly give them.

The whipping seemed to go on forever, but finally he tired, dropped his belt to the floor and approached her again. Ran his hands gently over the inflamed marks he had caused, unfastened her wrists. She wrapped her arms around his neck and whispered to him again. He shuddered and fell at her feet, his arms grasping her knees, his face buried in her thighs. She held his head and stroked his hair, still smiling, still glowing.

The excitement I had felt earlier drained away completely and left me empty, with only vague longing and loss to take its place. I was no longer a participant, but a voyeur, a witness to something that should have been private. Yet, from the expression on her face and the way he still knelt at her feet, I knew that to them it was private. There had been no crowd watching, no friend looking on in excitement and fear, nothing but what they had with each other.

Nan sighed. Stopped. Continued. "Then I got up to go to the ladies' room. When I came back they'd disappeared. I didn't see them for the rest of the evening."

I turned my head to the café window and looked out into the street. "What do you suppose happened next?"

Nan shrugged. "My guess is he took her back to some hotel and fucked her properly. At least that's what I hope happened. She deserved it." She took a drink of coffee. "I guess he did, too. Then I suspect he left."

"Probably." I nodded and reached into a pocket, pulling out my cigarettes. "Do you mind?" I asked.

Her mouth twisted into a grin. "Normally, yes, but I'll make an exception in this case, if you'll tell me ...."

"Tell you what?"

"Tell me what she said both times to make him react the way he did."

I lit my cigarette. Brushed a few tears away from my eyes. "That's an easy call and you shouldn't even have to ask. She said...." I paused and shook my head, suddenly tired of the storytelling game and wanting there to be no misunderstanding, "no. *I* said 'I love you.'"